"So the prince ...te affair," Jacques said, continuing the legend of Le Château d'Amour Inconnu. "And all summer she sang as she worked, a pure and beautiful sound that made even the doves sit still and listen."

Jessica held her breath. She felt herself transported to another world, a magical place of romance and passion.

"But one day Prince Frédéric was to be wed to a young marquise," Jacques said. "Torn between his love and his duty, Frédéric agonized day and night. But the preparations proceeded as planned. On the day of the wedding Isadora ran into the forest. And Frédéric ran into the woods after her."

"And so they lived happily ever after!" Jessica finished.

"Ah, no!" Jacques said, his face darkening. "This is a tragedy. Frédéric searched the woods, but the *belle* Isadora was nowhere to be seen. And so the marriage went on. But when Frédéric took his vows, a white dove appeared. It sang a sad song, and then it flew away. And it is said that on summer nights, the sweet and sorrowful sound of a dove can be heard."

"That's beautiful." Jessica sighed. "Maybe I'll hear the dove when I'm there."

Jacques winked. "Maybe you will have a mysterious love affair."

Visit the Official Sweet Valley Web Site on the Internet at:

http://www.sweetvalley.com

ONCE UPON
A TIME

Written by
Kate William

Created by
FRANCINE PASCAL

BANTAM BOOKS
NEW YORK · TORONTO · LONDON · SYDNEY · AUCKLAND

RL 6, age 12 and up

ONCE UPON A TIME
A Bantam Book / June 1997

Sweet Valley High® is a registered trademark of Francine Pascal.
Conceived by Francine Pascal.
Produced by Daniel Weiss Associates, Inc.
33 West 17th Street
New York, NY 10011.
Cover photography by Michael Segal.

ISBN: 0-553-57066-8

Published simultaneously in the United States and Canada

Bantam Books are published by Bantam Books, a division of Bantam
Doubleday Dell Publishing Group, Inc. Its trademark, consisting of the
words "Bantam Books" and the portrayal of a rooster, is Registered in U.S.
Patent and Trademark Office and in other countries. Marca Registrada.
Bantam Books, 1540 Broadway, New York, New York 10036.

PRINTED IN THE UNITED STATES OF AMERICA

OPM   0 9 8 7 6 5 4 3 2 1

To Chris Moustakis

Chapter 1

"Shampoo, conditioner, soap," sixteen-year-old Elizabeth Wakefield muttered to herself on Friday evening, throwing the last of her toiletries into her pink floral travel case.

She and her twin sister, Jessica, were leaving in the morning for the South of France, where they were spending the summer as au pairs for a royal European family. Jessica's best friend, Lila Fowler, was throwing a big going-away bash for the twins that evening, so they had to be ready to go before they left for the party.

Elizabeth put her hands on her hips and surveyed her bedroom. A large blue suitcase was packed and standing by the door, and her backpack was full to bursting. Her cream-colored room was neat and orderly. She had put away all her schoolbooks, and she had left a new message on her answering machine with her summer phone number. Everything seemed to be in order.

Elizabeth quickly performed a mental list, ticking off items in her mind. *Passport. Plane ticket. Traveler's checks. Journal.* Apparently she was all set to go. But still a nagging thought was bothering her. She felt as if she were forgetting something. What was it?

Then it hit her. *Todd.* She walked over to her dresser and tenderly picked up the framed photograph of her longtime boyfriend, Todd Wilkins.

Elizabeth gazed at the portrait of her handsome boyfriend. He was wearing his red Gladiators basketball jersey and a navy blue visor pulled low over his forehead. A few dark brown curls peeked out from underneath the cap, and his deep, coffee-colored brown eyes smiled at her warmly from the photo.

Elizabeth's heart fluttered as she read the words scrawled at the bottom. *To my good luck charm,* Todd had written. Elizabeth remembered exactly when she had taken the picture. It was the night of the championship basketball game in the fall, when Todd had scored the winning basket. "I couldn't have done it without you," he had whispered in her ear after the game. "You were my inspiration."

A sharp pang of regret hit Elizabeth. The thought of leaving Todd for so long was heartbreaking. They were going to be separated for a whole month, and it would be too expensive to make phone calls. And impossible to make weekend visits.

Elizabeth's chest tightened as she thought of

her upcoming separation from her boyfriend. She wondered if she'd have even a moment alone with Todd at Fowler Crest, Lila's father's mansion. She and Todd were sure to be surrounded by their friends all night.

Well, I'll just have to take him away from all that, Elizabeth decided as she slipped Todd's picture into the inside pocket of her shoulder bag. She resolved to leave Lila's party early and whisk Todd away to Miller's Point for a more private farewell. Miller's Point was a popular parking spot overlooking Sweet Valley, and it was Elizabeth and Todd's favorite place to go when they wanted to be alone.

Elizabeth sank down onto her bed. Tonight would be the last night that they would get to enjoy the beautiful view together. "It's going to be a long summer," she whispered wistfully.

Suddenly the door to the bathroom adjoining the twins' rooms flew open, and Jessica breezed in. Elizabeth looked up, startled.

Jessica bounded into the room, her whole body bursting with energy. She looked glamorous and sexy in a long, deep red cotton skirt with a cream-colored Lycra T-shirt. Her golden blond hair was swept up on her head, one long lock twisted into a curl over her forehead. Her blue-green eyes sparkled dramatically, and her cheeks were flushed pink with excitement.

Jessica put her hands on her hips. "Aren't you ready yet?" she demanded. "Lila said to come over around seven-thirty."

Elizabeth smiled wryly. Jessica was perpetually late, a quality that she tended to justify on the grounds that the party didn't start until she got there. "Since when are you concerned about the time?" Elizabeth asked.

"Since I'm the guest of honor—along with you, of course," Jessica replied. She picked up a compact disk from Elizabeth's bookshelf and spun it around on her index finger. "And if you don't hurry up, we're going to miss all the fun." The CD spun off Jessica's finger and sailed across the room. It hit the far wall and fell onto the bed.

"Jes-si-ca!" Elizabeth moaned, retrieving the CD and quickly putting it back in its case.

Now Jessica was rummaging around in Elizabeth's backpack. She pulled out a pair of rose-tinted sunglasses and pushed them up on her forehead. Then she began dancing around the room in an imitation of a waltz, singing an Edith Piaf song. Ever since Jessica had learned they were going to France, she had started to listen to French music obsessively even though she didn't understand the words.

"Quand il me prend dans ses bras, il me par-le tous bas, je vois la vie en ro-se," she crooned.

Elizabeth couldn't help laughing. "Hey, Jess, why don't you take some of that energy and use it to transport your hundred suitcases down the steps?"

"My bags! That's right!" Jessica ripped off the sunglasses and threw them back in Elizabeth's bag. Then she sped out the door.

Elizabeth shook her head as her hyperactive twin exited. Sometimes she couldn't believe she and Jessica were even related. Despite their identical appearance, from their sun-streaked blond hair to their aquamarine eyes to their slim, athletic figures, the girls couldn't be more different in character.

Jessica was thrilled to get away for the summer. There was nothing she liked better than change. Jessica went through boyfriends even faster than she went through social trends and clothing styles. If she sensed a moment of calm in Sweet Valley, Jessica was sure to stir things up. The cocaptain of the cheerleading squad and an active member of Pi Beta Alpha, the most exclusive sorority at Sweet Valley High, Jessica's energy was infectious. Whether on the sidelines of the football field, in the middle of the beach disco, or in the thick of the mall, Jessica always drew a crowd.

While Elizabeth had just as much energy as her sister, she directed it toward more internal pursuits. A staff writer for the *Oracle* and a straight-A student, Elizabeth had high aspirations to be a famous journalist one day. In her spare time she preferred quieter activities: taking a moonlight walk on the beach with Todd, going to a movie with her best friends, Enid Rollins and Maria Slater, or just sitting alone in the park, writing in her journal.

Unlike Jessica, Elizabeth hated it when her world was rocked. She had been looking forward to a peaceful, productive summer in which she could work on her writing and spend some quality time with Todd.

Elizabeth took one last look at the picture in her hand and her eyes narrowed in a scowl. "I can't believe I let Jessica talk me into taking this job," she grumbled to herself.

Recently their father had done some legal work for Children of the World, an international employment agency that specialized in educational and child care positions. One evening he had casually mentioned that an opening for an au pair position to the prince and princess de Sainte-Marie had suddenly become available. The royal family of a European principality was looking for somebody to take care of their children at their summer château on an island in the Mediterranean.

Jessica had nearly jumped out of her seat at the possibility of living with royalty, even though she didn't even know at the time what an au pair was.

"It's a fancy term for a live-in baby-sitter," Elizabeth had explained.

Her twin had remained undaunted. She had immediately put a plan into action with typical Jessica Wakefield energy and stubbornness. With lightning quick speed, she had gathered together an impressive portfolio, complete with a résumé, a cover letter, and letters of recommendation. A short time later she had been hired for the job. However, there had been one stipulation. Because Jessica was younger and less experienced than the

6

family desired, the agency had to find a second girl to share the duties.

That's when Jessica began working on Elizabeth—begging, cajoling, and threatening to drive Elizabeth insane if she didn't agree to join her. "It'll be an adventure," Jessica had said. "We'll get to live in the South of France." "We'll be able to practice our French." "We'll learn all about a foreign culture."

After two weeks of nonstop pressure Elizabeth had finally given in. *I should have put my foot down from the start,* she told herself as she hugged Todd's photo to her chest. Not only would she be away from Todd and her friends for months, she would also be giving up a chance to work at *Flair* magazine over the summer. She had recently served as the assistant to the managing editor of the famous fashion magazine as part of a two-week internship program. The editorial board had been so impressed with her work that they had offered her a summer position.

Elizabeth heaved a sigh as she zipped her shoulder bag shut. Instead of working in the editorial department for a renowned magazine, she was going to spend the summer *baby-sitting* on some deserted island in a foreign country. *Why can't I ever say no to my twin?* she thought in disgust.

Frowning, Elizabeth hoisted her backpack over her shoulders and picked up her suitcase. After nudging open her bedroom door, she lugged her bag down the hall and carried it downstairs to the foyer.

Jessica was standing by the front door, jingling the keys to the Jeep. "It's about time!" she exclaimed.

Elizabeth stumbled over a duffel bag on the floor and quickly steadied herself. Her mouth dropped open as she took in Jessica's bags, which were stacked by the door. Jessica had filled up a five-piece floral set of luggage, plus a dress bag and an oversize backpack.

"You planning to move to France permanently?" Elizabeth asked.

"Sorry, no time for small talk," Jessica responded cheerfully, nudging the door open with her foot. "The party is about to begin!"

Elizabeth shook her head as Jessica took her firmly by the shoulders and steered her through the door.

"You and Liz certainly can draw a crowd," Amy Sutton remarked to Jessica at Fowler Crest later that evening. It was 10 P.M., and the party was in full motion. The Droids, a popular rock group from Sweet Valley High, were playing on a raised dais on the back patio. Everyone was dancing, laughing, eating, and obviously having a great time.

Jessica laughed. "That's nice of you to say, but I think we should give Lila credit for this fab turnout."

Lila *had* really outdone herself this time. Jessica's best friend was famous for throwing lavish parties, and this one was no exception. But then, any event at Fowler Crest was always magnificent. The white,

Spanish-style mansion was surrounded by plush, sculptured lawns with Olympic-size tennis courts and a sparkling fountain. The back patio, with its red clay tiles, hanging baskets of plants, and tall lemon trees, was the perfect example of California beauty.

But tonight Fowler Crest was even more extravagant than usual. The patio was decorated with fresh flowers, tropical plants, and citronella lanterns. An elegant buffet table was set up, and black-tailed waiters were walking around with platters of hors d'oeuvres. A big banner reading Bon Voyage, Jessica and Elizabeth! hung over the patio.

It looks like everybody *in the junior class showed up!* Jessica thought with satisfaction. Ronnie Edwards and Aaron Dallas were trying to throw Sandra Bacon and Jean West into the pool, and the girls were shouting with laughter. Maria Slater and Olivia Davidson were surrounded by a group of admiring guys by the refreshment table. And Penny Ayala, Enid Rollins, and Ken Matthews were doing a crazy line dance across the dance floor, which was drawing lots of laughs.

From the moment she had arrived, Jessica had barely been able to take a breath. Every time she turned, it seemed like somebody else wanted to wish her well.

Usually Jessica was thrilled with this kind of attention, but for some reason the party tonight left her flat. She shifted impatiently, wishing she were already on the plane to France.

9

"Ah! Jessica! *Zere* you are!" a familiar voice from behind her called.

Jessica turned to see Winston Egbert approaching.

"Oh, boy," Amy said with a groan. "Get a load of Winston."

Affectionately known as the class clown, Winston was looking particularly ridiculous that evening. He was wearing a French-cut tuxedo jacket with sleeves that were too short, revealing his knobby wrists. A black French beret was pulled low over Winston's left eye, and a baguette was tucked under his arm.

Winston made a low, sweeping bow when he reached them. "*Bonsoir,* mesdemoiselles," he greeted them in French.

Amy giggled. "*Bonsoir,* Winston."

"Monsieur Eg-berrrt, eef you pleez," Winston corrected her.

Jessica couldn't help laughing at Winston's ex-aggerated French accent. "Winston, you are such a geek," she said.

"I eve brought you end your lovely seester a pre-sent," Winston said. "Where eez your ozer alf?"

My other half? Jessica pondered. Now that she thought about it, she hadn't seen her twin for a while. She had noticed Elizabeth and Todd slip away from the crowd about an hour ago, and they hadn't reappeared since. "I think she and Todd snuck off together."

"Ahh, too bad!" Winston exclaimed. "Pleez give

10

Leez my best weeshes." He held out a small white box with a big red bow wrapped around it.

Jessica untied the bow and lifted off the lid. A tiny pin with a little green frog on it was nestled in a bed of tissue paper. She shook her head with a smile, holding up the pin for Amy to see. "Winston, you are too much."

"It eez a French frog," Winston explained in mock seriousness.

Jessica nodded. "Yeah, I got it," she said. "Thanks, Winston, it's lovely."

Just then Dana Larson, the lead singer of the Droids, spoke into the microphone. "Hey, everybody, I'd like to introduce a brand-new song. It's called 'Solid Ice.' We hope you like it!" The band broke into a funky blues beat, and the crowd roared enthusiastically.

"Hey, let's dance!" Winston exclaimed.

"You go ahead," Jessica said, waving him away.

Jessica watched pensively as Winston joined the crowd on the dance floor. She had been thrilled about this party, and it had turned out to be even better than she had imagined. But still, she felt somehow disappointed. She couldn't quite put her finger on the reason for it. After all, she was lucky. She had really great friends, and they had all turned out to say good-bye.

Jessica bit her lip. *Obviously I'm ready for a change*, she thought.

        ❖   ❖   ❖

Elizabeth stood in Todd's arms on the Spanish-style veranda, gazing into the Fowlers' pool. The pool was filled with dozens of floating candles, which cast a melancholy yellow glow along the surface of the water. The tiny flickering lights seemed to reflect her somber mood.

Elizabeth leaned back against Todd's chest and pulled his arms tighter around her. "We won't get to spend much time at Baywater this summer," she said sadly. Baywater was a deserted strand of beach that had become Elizabeth and Todd's private haven. They often went there on summer nights for moonlight picnics.

"I know," Todd responded. "It's weird. In just twenty-four hours you're going to be staring out at the Mediterranean Sea."

Elizabeth sighed. The thought didn't excite her at all. Her chest felt tight, and she was on the verge of tears. She didn't know what had come over her, but ever since the au pair job had become a reality, all she could think about was Todd. *Maybe it takes a separation to make you realize how much you appreciate someone,* she thought.

"I wish I weren't going," Elizabeth declared.

Todd murmured in agreement.

Elizabeth turned and took both of Todd's hands in hers. She looked up into his familiar deep brown eyes, which gleamed warmly in the light of the candles, and her heart skipped a beat. "I love you, Todd," Elizabeth whispered in a throaty voice.

"I love you too," Todd said quickly.

"And I promise to write every single day," Elizabeth continued, feeling a tear come to her eye. "Maybe we can call each other a few times too."

Todd nodded, but his eyes darted away from her.

Elizabeth frowned and blinked back her tears. Todd seemed distinctly uncomfortable. In fact, he had been acting odd all evening. "Todd? Is something wrong?" she asked.

Todd coughed, but he shook his head quickly.

"OK, you don't have to write every day," Elizabeth joked. "You can write every *other* day." She laughed nervously, waiting for Todd to join in. But his expression remained serious.

Now Elizabeth was really concerned. "Todd, is there something you'd like to tell me?" Her breathing quickened.

Todd swallowed hard and glanced away. "Yeah," he muttered. "There is." He took a deep breath and stared at the ground.

After a moment's silence Todd cleared his throat. "Elizabeth, we need to talk."

"Having fun, Jess?" Lila asked, heading up to Jessica with a plate of appetizers in her hand. Lila looked particularly elegant in a loose-fitting black silk pantsuit. The jacket tapered in at the waist, and the pant legs flared out at the ankles. Her long brown hair was tied back at the nape of her neck with a wine-colored silk scarf.

Jessica shrugged. "The party is nice."

"*Nice?*" Lila echoed, obviously miffed at the bland praise.

"It's a fantastic party," Jessica amended.

"That's better." Lila sniffed. She picked up a cheese-filled pastry puff and popped it into her mouth. "Mmm," she murmured appreciatively. Then she held her plate out to Jessica. "Want one?" she offered.

Jessica shook her head. "No, I don't have much of an appetite."

Lila shrugged and jabbed her fork into a stuffed mushroom. "What's *with* you tonight?"

"I just can't wait to get out of Sweet Valley," Jessica explained. "I feel like I've been dancing with the same ten cute guys my whole life."

Lila sighed. "I know what you mean. Every year this school seems to get smaller and smaller." She lifted her fork and took a bite of the mushroom.

"That's exactly it!" Jessica agreed. "We've been around here for too long. It's time for a change." She smiled, feeling excited again. "I know France is going to be absolutely wonderful."

Lila shook her head. "I wouldn't get your hopes up, Jess. It may sound exotic, but Europe isn't that different from America. I've been to France a hundred times. Guys there are like guys everywhere— fun for a while, but ultimately disappointing."

Jessica knew that her friend's attitude had a lot to do with her frustration with her current boyfriend, Bo Creighton, a guy she had met while she and Jessica had been junior counselors at Camp Echo Mountain, a performing arts camp in the mountains of Montana.

Bo was a cute guy from a wealthy D.C. family, and Lila had fallen head over heels in love with him. They had been inseparable at camp and had even managed to keep up a long-distance relationship for a few months. But Bo's calls and letters had started to drop off, and Lila was getting discouraged.

Jessica shrugged. "You can be as negative as you want," she replied. "But I plan to fall in love with a prince and have the time of my life."

"I hate to break it to you, but you won't be in much of a position to find a prince," Lila remarked. "You're going to be cooped up with a bunch of royal European brats." Lila brushed back an errant strand of hair with a carefully manicured nail. "Being an au pair is *not* glamorous."

Jessica smiled, but she didn't say anything. She wasn't about to let Lila spoil a single moment of her anticipation. This was going to be a summer she'd never forget. She could feel it in her bones.

Elizabeth's heart fluttered nervously as Todd led her to a bench under a huge oak tree on the Fowlers' landscaped grounds. A light wind whistled gently through the leaves, and she could hear the faint sounds of the party in the distance.

Todd sat down and faced her, his face pale.

15

"Well, I . . . *uh* . . ." He coughed. "I've been think-ing. . . ." Todd's voice trailed off, and he stood up. Then he walked in a small circle and sat down again.

Elizabeth's heart began pounding in alarm. Obviously Todd had something important to tell her. And she had a feeling she wasn't going to like what she was about to hear.

"Yes?" Elizabeth prompted him.

"Well, it's just, it's just—I'm worried about this separation," Todd blurted suddenly. "We know from past experience that long-distance relation-ships are hard to maintain."

Elizabeth let out her breath in a rush, over-come with relief. She had been expecting some horrible news, but Todd was just nervous about being apart from her as well. And she knew to what he was referring. When Todd had moved away to Vermont temporarily, Elizabeth had gotten involved with his best friend, Ken Matthews. Elizabeth and Ken had kept their brief affair a se-cret for a long time, but eventually the truth had come out. Todd had been devastated. In time, though, he had forgiven her, and their relationship had grown even stronger after that.

Elizabeth weighed her words carefully. "I un-derstand what you're worried about, but this isn't really a long-distance relationship," she said. "It's just for the summer."

"So was Camp Echo Mountain," Todd pointed out, reminding Elizabeth of the time she spent working as a junior counselor in the mountains of Montana. Elizabeth's face burned at the memory. Although neither one mentioned her brief fling with a senior counselor there, the name *Joey Mason* seemed to hang in the air between them.

"That was different," Elizabeth insisted quickly, but she stared down at the ground. That wasn't much of an argument.

"If anything, this is worse," Todd responded. "You're going to be practically on the other side of the world, meeting all kinds of exotic guys."

Elizabeth bit her lip. She had known that her affair with Joey Mason would come back to haunt her someday. Todd had claimed he'd forgiven her, but obviously that wasn't true. Elizabeth looked at him with imploring eyes. "Todd, I promise I would never cheat on you again," she said, her voice catching in her throat.

Todd nodded. "I know that," he said softly.

Elizabeth shook her head, feeling tears of frustration come to her eyes. "No, you don't," she insisted. Elizabeth kicked at a leaf on the ground. "You don't trust me anymore."

"It's not that," Todd responded. "I *do* trust you. I just don't think it's fair to you. You should be able to go out with anyone you want while you're in France."

Elizabeth frowned, suddenly suspicious of Todd's self-sacrificial air. Since when was her boyfriend concerned about *her* freedom to see other guys? "And what about you?" Elizabeth

17

threw back at him. "I suppose you're anxious to start dating other girls."

Todd shrugged. "I wouldn't exactly say *anxious*," he responded carefully. "But I do think we should let each other loose for the summer."

Todd's words hit her like a ton of bricks. Obviously he didn't care about her feelings at all. He just wanted his freedom. Elizabeth felt a tiny fist gripping her heart.

"Just for the summer, Todd?" she retorted.

Todd gently squeezed her hand. "I don't want to lose you, Elizabeth. I hope you'll come back to me. We could reevaluate our relationship at the end of the summer."

Elizabeth yanked her hand away. "And what if I don't *want* to come back to you?" she snapped.

Todd's jaw clenched, and he sighed. "I guess that's a chance I'll have to take," he replied.

Elizabeth could hardly believe what she was hearing. "You've already decided all this, haven't you?" she asked, her eyes flashing angrily.

Todd didn't respond, but the pained look in his brown eyes provided the answer. Elizabeth realized that he had already made his decision and that there was nothing she could do to change his mind.

Elizabeth stood up slowly, blinking back tears. "Well, don't worry," she said quietly. "You can have all the freedom you want. *Forever.*"

With that she turned and walked away with all the dignity she could muster.

"Elizabeth, wait!" Todd called from behind her.

Elizabeth could feel her eyes burning. "Leave me alone!" she yelled. She slipped off her sandals and grabbed the straps in one hand. Then she ran as if a demon were after her. Barely able to see through her tears, she crossed the manicured lawns, sprinted around a tennis court, and raced toward the circular front driveway.

As she was running toward the Jeep, parked in front of the mansion, she heard the sound of Todd's footsteps chasing her. "Liz, wait!" he shouted. "Liz! Come back!"

Panting, Elizabeth reached the Jeep and yanked open the driver's-side door. "Leave me alone!" she yelled over her shoulder to Todd. She jumped in the car and slammed the door shut. But Todd reached her just as she was revving the engine.

"Elizabeth, be reasonable," Todd pleaded through the open window. "Just because I think we should give each other freedom for a while doesn't mean that I don't love you."

"Yes, it does," Elizabeth replied hotly. "I never want to speak to you again."

She jerked the Jeep into gear and backed out of the Fowlers' driveway, tears streaming down her face.

Chapter 2

"Bonjour, je m'appelle Jessica," Jessica chanted into the mirror above her bureau on Saturday morning. *"Comment allez-vous? Je vais très bien."* She smiled charmingly into the mirror, letting the dimple in her left cheek deepen.

Jessica pranced around the room, her heart bursting with excitement. She'd been up since dawn, rushing around the house to get ready. But even though she had barely gotten any sleep, she was wide awake. Not only were she and Elizabeth really going to spend the summer in the South of France, but they were going to be living with royalty—a real prince and a princess.

The only problem was Elizabeth. She hadn't stopped crying for more than five minutes since the party the night before. Jessica had tried to comfort her when she had gotten home, but her sister had been inconsolable. She had finally fallen into a troubled sleep around two in the morning.

Jessica furrowed her brow worriedly. She hoped Elizabeth was feeling better this morning. She didn't want anything preventing their departure for France.

She walked through the bathroom adjoining their rooms and knocked lightly on the door. There was no answer. Jessica hesitated, then knocked again.

"Come in," her sister replied in a wooden voice.

Jessica pushed open the door. Elizabeth was sitting on the edge of the bed, still in her nightgown. She was staring into space with a hairbrush in her hand, and her eyes were red and swollen. A big box of blue tissues sat by her side. Jessica frowned. It wasn't like her sister to fall totally to pieces.

"Lizzie, we're going to *Europe* today!" Jessica exclaimed, trying to infuse some excitement into her twin. She plopped down next to Elizabeth on the bed.

Elizabeth just scowled.

"I know you like to dress casual, but don't you think the occasion calls for something a bit more formal?" Jessica piped up.

Elizabeth cracked a smile, then she burst into tears.

Jessica wrapped an arm around her sister, feeling a little desperate. "Elizabeth, if you keep this up, you're going to flood the room," she chided her gently.

Elizabeth nodded, but her sobs just increased. Jessica hugged her tightly and rocked her back and forth. Finally Elizabeth's sobs subsided. She hiccuped and reached for the box of tissues by her side.

"Our plane leaves in three hours, Liz," Jessica pointed out. Elizabeth nodded and wiped her damp cheeks with edge of her pillowcase. "It's just that . . . when Todd . . ." Her voice broke on a sob.

"Shhh, I know," Jessica said, rubbing her sister's back. "Try not to think about it for now." She paused, then she spoke softly. "We'd better go downstairs because Steven and Billie came home last night just to see us off. And Mom and Dad are downstairs cooking a special farewell breakfast."

Elizabeth cried even harder. She pulled out a tissue and blew her nose loudly. "I just *knew* this trip would be a big mistake," she said through her tears.

"What are you talking about?" Jessica protested. "You and I are going to have the best time ever."

Elizabeth scowled and twirled a finger in the air. "La-di-da," she said. She pulled her pillow into her lap and wrapped her arms around it. "I don't feel like ever leaving my room again." She sniffed.

Jessica sighed and stood up. Clearly she wasn't helping matters. "Listen, I think you need some time alone to get yourself together. I'll come back to check on you in a few minutes, OK?"

Elizabeth nodded, but she kept staring fixedly at the wall.

Jessica headed back to her room, feeling discouraged. She could cheerfully murder Todd for upsetting her twin right before their trip. Of course, Jessica personally thought it was a good idea for Elizabeth to have a little breathing room. She'd been dating Todd since the Stone Age, and he was even less interesting than a caveman.

Jessica checked her hair and makeup in the full-length mirror. She looked bright and lovely. She had been wearing a light cotton dress, but her mother had insisted she change. "It'll get cold on the plane," Alice Wakefield had said. So now Jessica had on a pair of chic beige linen pants and a black blazer. Her hair hung in loose golden waves around her face. Jessica paced around her empty room. Finally she crossed through the bathroom to her sister's room.

Elizabeth was still sitting on the bed, holding the hairbrush. "Uh-oh," Jessica muttered under her breath. "This is getting serious."

Jessica sat down beside her twin and gently squeezed her hands. "Elizabeth, you *have* to get yourself together," she insisted. At this rate she was worried that Elizabeth would back out of their trip completely.

"I know," Elizabeth replied tearfully.

Jessica decided to appeal to Elizabeth's intellectual interests. "Think of how much we're going to *learn* this summer. France is full of history and culture." *And cute guys,* she added silently.

Elizabeth shrugged. "I don't care," she said.

Finally Jessica lost her patience. "Elizabeth

Wakefield, what has gotten into you?" she scolded. "You've never been one to let a guy get in the way of your intellectual interests." Jessica stood up and crossed the carpet as she lectured her sister. "This is a chance in a million. We're going to be living in the midst of real culture, and we're going to learn a foreign language." Jessica paused for a moment. "You know, if Todd can't handle a one-month separation, then he isn't the person you thought he was."

Elizabeth sat up straighter. She seemed to be weighing Jessica's words. Finally she managed a smile. "You're right," she said firmly. "I'm going to use this summer to put Todd behind me—once and for all."

Jessica breathed a sigh of relief. She didn't know what exactly she had said to turn her sister around, but she was glad it had worked. "Now hurry up and get ready before Steven eats all the pancakes!"

Half an hour later Elizabeth dragged herself down the stairs. Despite her resolve, she couldn't stop thinking about Todd. Her legs felt as though they weighed two tons each. She had showered and put on a fresh pair of jeans, but she didn't feel any better. She could hear everybody laughing and chatting at the breakfast table, and the aroma of blueberry pancakes and fresh-roasted coffee wafted up the steps.

Elizabeth groaned. She didn't know how she

was going to face her family. She was tempted to head up the stairs and climb back into bed. The last thing she felt like doing was enduring a big Wakefield family farewell . . . or taking a long plane ride to meet some old-fashioned royalty . . . or spending a lonely summer in France. . . .

Sighing, Elizabeth turned the corner into the kitchen.

"There she is!" Steven cried. "Sleeping beauty!" Steven, the twins' older brother, was flipping pancakes at the stove, a white apron tied around his waist. Billie Winkler, his girlfriend from Sweet Valley University, was standing next to him, mixing batter. Billie looked fresh and beautiful as usual. She was wearing faded blue jeans and a teal-colored T-shirt, and her silky chestnut hair hung loose around her shoulders.

"We were worried you were going to sleep through your flight," Billie chimed in.

"I wish I had," Elizabeth muttered under her breath.

"Is something wrong, honey?" Mrs. Wakefield asked from the table.

Elizabeth shook her head and slipped into her seat. "Just tired," she mumbled, averting her gaze.

"The party went on until pretty late last night," Jessica piped up. "It was really great. The food was incredible, and almost *everybody* showed up. Winston Egbert was dressed like a typical French guy, with a tuxedo jacket and a beret. He gave us a

French frog as a gift." Jessica held up the tiny green pin, and everybody laughed.

Elizabeth gave her twin a small smile, grateful for her efforts to divert their parents' attention.

Steven came to the table with a plate of steaming pancakes and flipped a few onto Elizabeth's plate.

"Thanks, Steven," Elizabeth mumbled. She picked up her fork and obligatorily cut into a pancake. Blueberry pancakes were Steven's specialty, and these were done to perfection. But they tasted like sandpaper to Elizabeth. She forced herself to chew and swallow, and quickly gulped down some orange juice.

"When does our plane leave?" Jessica asked suddenly. "What time is it? Are we late? Are the bags in the car?"

"Whoa!" Ned Wakefield said with a smile, holding up a hand. "The car is all loaded up, and we've got plenty of time. Now eat your breakfast. You'll need all your strength for the trip."

Jessica made a face but picked up a piece of toast and bit into it.

Mrs. Wakefield shook her head. "Well, even if you two aren't sad to leave, we're going to miss you terribly this summer," she said.

Prince Albert, the Wakefields' golden retriever, came bounding to the table. "Arf! Arf! Arf!" he chimed in.

"Atta boy!" Steven said, patting him on the side.

While her family discussed the details of their

27

trip, Elizabeth's attention wandered to the phone. It was hanging innocently on the wall, mocking her with its silence. Despite the fact that she'd told Todd she never wanted to speak to him again, Elizabeth expected him to call this morning. She couldn't help hoping that he would admit that he'd made a terrible mistake and didn't want to break up with her for the summer.

Of course, Elizabeth thought stubbornly, *I would absolutely refuse to go out with him this summer. There's no way I'd forgive him for last night.*

Still, said a little voice in her head, *he could at least make an effort.*

But a half an hour later, when everybody was heading out the door, the phone still hadn't rung. Elizabeth was shocked. She had been sure Todd would call her to apologize, or at least to wish her well. Pain squeezed her heart.

Elizabeth was quiet on the way to the airport, feeling nostalgic as she watched the familiar winding streets of Sweet Valley go by. Fortunately nobody seemed to notice her mood. Jessica was cheerful and animated enough for both of them.

When her father turned onto the coastal highway, Elizabeth could see the foamy Pacific Ocean glittering green in the distance. Jumbled memories flooded into her mind: swimming with Todd in the ocean, playing volleyball with him on the beach, having a moonlight picnic at Baywater, walking barefoot hand in hand on the sand. . . .

Elizabeth felt a pang of sadness. Each sight they passed seemed to have sentimental value for her. And each step was taking her farther and farther away from Todd.

Even when the family was at the airport, waiting for the twins' flight to be announced, Elizabeth couldn't help scanning the crowd for Todd's face.

Her family was talking animatedly in the background; loud voices were announcing flights over the loudspeaker in different languages; well-dressed businessmen and businesswomen hurried by with briefcases tucked under their arms. But it was all a blur for Elizabeth. All she could think of was Todd.

"Flight 786, now boarding!" boomed an announcement.

Jessica squealed and jumped up and down. "That's our flight!" she exclaimed.

Mrs. Wakefield was teary eyed as she hugged them good-bye. "What will I do without you two for the whole summer?" she asked.

"You'll get some rest!" Jessica quipped.

"That's for sure!" Mr. Wakefield said with a grin. "You two are quite a handful!"

"Use the phone whenever you want!" Steven interjected jokingly.

Jessica made a face at him, then giggled.

"Girls, do you have your tickets?" Mrs. Wakefield asked nervously.

The twins nodded.

"And your passports?"

"Yes, Mom," they said in unison.

"Oh, dear, this is harder than I had thought," Mrs. Wakefield said, her eyes clouding over. "Remember, don't talk to any strangers. Write to us often! Make sure you eat properly! Look out for each other!"

"And have a good time!" Mr. Wakefield said with a wink.

Jessica giggled again, and the girls hugged him good-bye.

"Bon voyage!" Steven called.

"Have a wonderful time!" Billie added.

"C'mon, Liz!" Jessica exclaimed, grabbing her sister's hand.

Elizabeth followed her, her heart heavy. She turned back and looked at the crowd. Steven, Billie, and Mr. Wakefield waved, and Mrs. Wakefield blew her a kiss.

Elizabeth waved back, scanning the crowd quickly. But there was no sign of Todd.

Hours later Elizabeth gazed absently out the airplane window, still dwelling on Todd's hurtful words. She couldn't believe Todd wanted to date other girls. After all the time they'd been together, Todd wanted his freedom. He was sick of her.

Their final words from the night before echoed in her mind. *And what if I don't want to come back to you? That's a chance I'll have to take.* Elizabeth squeezed her eyes shut, fighting back tears. If

Todd was willing to risk losing her, one thing was crystal clear—he didn't love her anymore.

The plane was packed, but it was pretty calm. The flight attendants had served an early chicken dinner, and then the passengers had watched a movie. Now everybody was sleeping or reading quietly. The only lights on in the plane were tiny overhead beams. Next to her Jessica was curled up in a blanket, sound asleep. Even though she had slept fitfully the night before, Elizabeth was wide awake.

Elizabeth bit her lip, trying to make sense of her and Todd's breakup. Maybe it was really her fault. After all, she *had* cheated on Todd with Joey Mason. She had broken their trust. Elizabeth squinted, remembering a saying Maria had once recited to her: "Trust is like a crystal vase. Once it's shattered, it's broken forever."

But I really believed Todd had forgiven me, Elizabeth thought. She drew her knees up to her chest and wrapped her arms around them. Something just didn't make sense. It seemed like Todd was just searching for an excuse to break up with her. Was he interested in someone else? Was he just waiting for her to get on the plane so he could date another girl? If so, who was it?

No, Elizabeth thought with certainty. *This isn't an issue of trust. Or self-sacrifice.* Todd wasn't concerned about her feelings at all. He just wanted his freedom. It was as simple as that. *He probably has a date lined up for tonight already,* she thought.

Elizabeth sighed and leaned her head back against the headrest. She had been turning the same thoughts around in her mind for hours, and she wasn't getting anywhere. She had to focus on something else. She fumbled through her backpack and took out *The Baby-sitter's Guide to Children,* a book she had bought as soon as she'd given in to Jessica's plan. Concentrating on her future charges would help take her mind off Todd. Besides, it never hurt to be prepared.

Elizabeth turned to the first page, but then she sighed again. Worrying about baby-sitting wasn't the best alternative to thinking about Todd. The thought of spending an entire summer as an au pair made her stomach turn.

Even though Elizabeth loved children, she'd had a bad experience with kids at Camp Echo Mountain. Her ten-year-old charges had hated her and had dubbed her "Dizzy Lizzie," a name that had caught on with the whole camp. Elizabeth's face burned at the humiliating memory.

Then Elizabeth shook her head hard. *This time will be different,* she decided. *This time I'll be ready.* She returned to her book with determination and opened to the table of contents. The twins would be taking care of three children, aged three, five, and six. Elizabeth flipped to the chapters that dealt with these ages specifically.

"Six-year-olds can be a handful," Elizabeth read. *"They are full of energy and surprises. . . ."*

But as she read, her eyes began to droop. Slowly she fell into a deep sleep.

Flowers . . . Elizabeth was surrounded by fields of wildflowers. As she walked, the fragrance enveloped her. The sun was warm on her skin. Spellbound, she drew in a deep breath. Southern France was almost as beautiful as her own Sweet Valley.

But suddenly she realized she was lost. The path she had followed had disappeared. For miles around her all she could see was acres of wildflowers—and the sky, which was rapidly turning gray. It would be dark soon. Elizabeth began to panic.

Then, out of nowhere, a gorgeous guy with jet-black hair and deep blue eyes rode up on a white stallion. In one smooth movement he leaned over and lifted her up onto his horse. Elizabeth wrapped her arms around his lean, muscular waist. Her heart beat wildly as they rode off into the sunset. . . .

Elizabeth woke up with a start.

"Sorry," Jessica said with a giggle. She was searching through Elizabeth's backpack. "I was looking for your French-English dictionary. I was trying to be very quiet."

"No problem," Elizabeth mumbled. *It was a ridiculous dream anyway,* she added silently. *I've already discovered that my prince is really a frog.*

Chapter 3

"This is a very famous café," Louis Landeau remarked on Sunday morning to his eighteen-year-old son, Jacques. He spoke in the slow, lilting French typical of natives of the South of France. Jacques and Louis were having a leisurely breakfast at Les Deux Magots, a well-known café on the Boulevard Saint-Germain in Paris.

Louis made a sweeping gesture with his hand, indicating the dark interior of the refined café. "Jean-Paul Sartre and Simone de Beauvoir used to be regulars here," he said. "Some of their most heated philosophical debates took placed in this very spot."

"Really?" Jacques asked, his interest piqued. "The existentialists?" His father was always full of little-known facts. No matter where they traveled, his father seemed to know something about the history or culture of the area.

Louis nodded. "And the existentialist slogan was 'existence precedes essence.'"

Jacques frowned. "What does that mean?" he asked. He picked up his coffee cup and took a sip of his café au lait.

"That means that we are the sum total of what we *do*," his father explained, a twinkle in his eyes. "In other words, 'to be is to act.'"

Jacques recognized the glint in his father's eyes. Louis Landeau was certainly a man of action. For him life had two purposes: finances and women. He spent most of his time chasing after one or the other.

Sure enough, his father leaned over to speak to a tall, well-dressed blond woman seated by the window. A cup of espresso sat in front of her and a newspaper was laid out on the table. She had a mildly bored expression on her pale face.

"Excuse me, but do you mind if I pose a slightly indiscreet question?" Louis asked.

The woman looked up, obviously grateful for the distraction. "That depends on the question," she responded with a slight smile.

Jacques Landeau stifled a grin as his father flirted with the young woman. Even though his father was in his fifties, he looked as elegant as ever. His dark hair was just graying around the temples, giving him a distinguished look, and his tanned face contrasted sharply with his light blue eyes. Despite the passage of time, his father still had an uncanny knack for charming females.

"You wouldn't by any chance be related to Catherine Deneuve?" Louis asked. "You have a striking resemblance to her."

The woman blushed, obviously flattered by the comparison to the beautiful French actress. Then she laughed and regained her self-composure. "I am related to Catherine Deneuve as much as you are related to President Chirac."

"Ah! Touché!" his father said, expressing his appreciation of her wit. He raised his glass to her. "I see I have met my equal."

The woman laughed, her slate gray eyes dancing. Then she waved him away with a flick of her wrist and went back to her paper.

Louis turned back to his son, his face full of good humor. "You're never too old for love," he said in a philosophical tone. He reached for another croissant from the bread basket in the middle of the table.

Jacques smiled in response, even though he knew that his father's attitude was mostly false bravado. His father certainly appreciated women, but inside he was lonely for one woman: his wife, who had left him years ago.

Jacques's mother had died when he was just a little boy, and he barely remembered her. He had a vague memory of a tall, graceful blond woman with a charming smile. Louis had never been able to replace her. Still, Jacques couldn't help hoping that his father would fall in love again and settle down with somebody else.

Louis sat back in his chair and bit into his croissant. Suddenly he was taken by a fit of coughing. Choking and sputtering, he leaned over and gasped for air. His breath came in short starts and his face turned bright red.

"Father, are you OK?" Jacques asked worriedly, leaning forward in concern.

His father nodded, but he continued to choke and cough.

"Here, have some water," Jacques said. He quickly poured a glass from the carafe in the middle of the table and handed it to him.

His father gave him a grateful smile and took a long gulp of water. His coughing eventually quieted down, and his face returned to its normal color. "Ahem!" Louis said, clearing his throat. "Too much rich living, eh, son?"

Jacques smiled and nodded, hiding his concern. He knew that his father was getting older and wouldn't be able to keep up their current lifestyle forever. The nonstop traveling wasn't good for him. They were constantly on the move—hopping a plane from one country to the next, shuffling from one hotel to another, dining in foreign restaurants and cafés. . . . Louis needed a place he could call home, and so did Jacques.

The winter before, Louis had suffered a bout of the flu that left him weak for nearly a month. The flu had turned into a serious case of pneumonia, and it had been touch and go for a while. After he had given him a clean bill of health, the doctor had warned Louis to take it easy. "If you don't settle down soon, your body is going to do it for you," the doctor warned him sternly.

"Of course, Doctor," his father had hastily agreed. The next day they were back on the road.

Jacques sighed, remembering the promise he had made to himself back then. He had vowed to find a way to help his father establish a life that was better for his health. And he had to do it before the summer was over. His father couldn't handle another long European winter.

Jacques stirred his café au lait pensively. His father needed a house of his own, with a garden where he could sit on sunny days and a cook to prepare healthy meals. Their place would have to be close to the city so his father wouldn't be bored and restless.

Maybe we could get a dog to accompany father on his walks, Jacques reflected, *and a handyman to keep up the place.* After all, neither Jacques or Louis knew anything about plumbing or carpentry. . . .

Only one question remained. *How am I going to manage all that?* Jacques wondered.

"Attention! Nous vous prions de ne pas laisser vos bagages sans surveillance!" a female voice boomed over the loudspeaker system. *"Ne vous séparez pas de vos bagages!"*

"What'd she say?" Jessica asked Elizabeth as they

made their way through the crowded Paris train station early Sunday morning. Jessica's duffel bag slipped off her shoulder and she adjusted it, jumping to shift the weight of her backpack. Wringing out her aching hands, she picked up the straps of her three suitcases and tugged them forward.

"She said not to leave your bags unattended," Elizabeth translated, walking along lightly beside her. "I guess it's a precaution against terrorist bombs."

Jessica nodded, unconcerned. The last thing she was worried about was bombs. All she cared about for the moment was getting to the train and getting her bags on it.

They reached the end of the corridor and came to a series of flashing signs. Jessica blinked and tried to make out the directions. "Gare du Nord, Gare de l'Est, Gare d'Austerlitz, métro, RER, TGV . . ." Jessica racked her brains, trying to recall her French vocabulary. *Gare* meant train station, and the *métro* was the subway system. But what was an *RER?* And what was a *TGV?*

Jessica sighed in frustration. She felt completely and utterly helpless. Everything was in French: the loudspeaker announcements, the signs, the conversations swirling around her. . . . She felt as if she were swimming underwater in a surreal dream. Or a nightmare.

Jessica had traveled in the past, and she had even spent some time in England as an intern at the *London Times*. But still, it seemed strange to be in the midst of a non-English-speaking crowd. Now she wished she had paid more attention in Ms. Dalton's French class. Of course, Elizabeth had managed to use *her* French to get them a cab from the airport to the train station.

Jessica wriggled out of her backpack and let it drop to the ground with a thud. "What now?" she asked, stretching out her aching neck.

Elizabeth was busy consulting their tickets. "I think we should go that way, to track six," she said, pointing to an archway on the left. "We're taking the train to the South of France."

"The *TGV?*" Jessica inquired.

"No, that's the *train à grande vitesse,*" Elizabeth explained. "It's superfast. I think we're taking a normal train."

Suddenly the loudspeaker crackled and a modulated female voice came over the system. *"Votre attention, s'il vous plaît. Il y a un changement de dernière minute. Le train numéro quatre-vingt dix-huit à destination de Nice partira de la voie trois. Attention au départ!"*

Jessica hoisted her backpack over her shoulders and turned in the direction of track 6. "Well, let's get going," she said.

"Wait!" Elizabeth cautioned, holding up an index finger. "I think she's talking about our train."

The message repeated itself. *"Voie trois— départ du train numéro quatre-vingt dix-huit."*

"Ninety-eight," Elizabeth said. "That's our train."

"Ninety-eight?" Jessica repeated. "But she didn't say ninety-eight."

Elizabeth nodded impatiently. "Yes, she did. Four times twenty plus eighteen. Ninety-eight."

"The French don't know how to count," Jessica grumbled.

"Maybe you should have studied a little harder in Ms. Dalton's class," Elizabeth said pointedly.

Jessica made a face, but before she could retort, a little man in a suit shuffled up to them. He was wearing a toupee that was in disarray, revealing a bald spot on the top of his head.

"Excusez-moi," he said to Jessica, a frazzled look on his face. *"Est-ce que vous avez l'heure, s'il vous plaît?"*

Jessica looked back at him, trying to digest his words. *"Parlez-vous anglais?"* she asked finally, asking him if he spoke English.

"L'heure!" he repeated loudly, pointing at his wrist frantically. *"L'heure!"*

Elizabeth smiled graciously and glanced at her watch. *"Il est trois heures,"* she said.

"Merci, mademoiselle," the man thanked her with a little bow. Then he hurried off.

Elizabeth smiled a little self-satisfied smile. Jessica rolled her eyes, disgusted with her sister's preening attitude.

"Jess, c'mon," Elizabeth urged her. "We've got to go to track three now. We're going to miss our train at this rate." She rushed off to the archway to the right.

Jessica picked up her suitcase straps and hurried after her sister. She groaned as one of the straps slipped out of her sweaty hand. Suddenly the biggest suitcase toppled over and fell onto its side. A wheel popped off and rolled away.

Jessica put her hands to her head. Now she was going to have to carry the suitcase, and every part of her body was screaming out in pain. Her back was in knots, her shoulders ached, her neck was tight, and even her hands hurt.

Jessica clenched her jaw and picked up the suitcase, dragging the other two bags in her left hand. Suddenly both suitcases fell over with a clatter and her garment bag slid onto the floor on top of them.

"Liz, will you stop for a minute!" Jessica shouted.

Elizabeth turned around, obviously annoyed.

"It would be a lot easier if you would carry one of my suitcases," Jessica said. "Take the small one." After all, Elizabeth only had one suitcase and her backpack to carry.

"No way," Elizabeth responded, walking back in her direction.

"Elizabeth, *please*," Jessica whined. "I simply can't—"

But Elizabeth cut her off. "Absolutely not," she said in a firm voice. "You're the one who talked me into coming on this trip. You can carry your own bags." Elizabeth crossed her arms over her chest. "Besides, you shouldn't have brought so much stuff," she added.

Jessica uttered an exasperated sigh. Elizabeth was in her "Miss Perfect" mode. She was even wearing comfortable shoes. Jessica, on the other hand, had on her gorgeous new Italian sandals, which were pinching her toes and cutting off the circulation in her feet.

"Fine," Jessica retorted, gritting her teeth and picking up her bags.

But ten minutes later she stopped again. She simply could not carry her big suitcase one moment longer. Her arm muscles were aching, and she was beginning to get blisters on her palms. "Elizabeth, we're going to have to find a cart."

Elizabeth put her hands on her hips. "I told you that you shouldn't have packed for a year."

Jessica tapped a foot impatiently. "Look, there's nothing I can do about it now. Can you just find out where we can get a cart?"

"You know, I don't know why *I* should have to take care of everything," Elizabeth said huffily. "We both took the same French classes, and we're both going to spend the summer in France." Elizabeth flipped her ponytail in annoyance. "You're going to have to make an effort sooner or later."

Jessica exhaled loudly. Clearly Elizabeth wasn't going to be any help. Jessica was going to have to test out her rusty French. Sighing, she stopped a passing woman. She was young, with frizzy red hair and a pointed nose.

Jessica searched her mind for the translation of

"I'm looking for a cart." "*Pardonnez-moi. Je cherche une carte,*" she said hesitantly.

The woman narrowed her eyes. "*Une tarte?*" she asked.

Jessica felt like screaming in frustration. "*Des* cartes," she repeated.

"*Vous voulez jouer aux cartes?*" the woman asked, looking surprised.

Elizabeth laughed out loud. "She thinks you want to play cards."

At this, Jessica practically exploded. "Liz, it's not funny. Can you *please* tell me how to say *cart* in French?"

Elizabeth shrugged. "I have no idea."

"*Merci,*" Jessica said to the woman, beginning to despair.

The woman gave them an odd smile and walked away.

Elizabeth glanced at her watch. "Look, Jess, we've really got to hurry. If we see a cart, we'll grab one. But for now we've got to haul these ourselves."

Jessica sighed and picked up her suitcases again. As she started to lug her bags forward a cute young guy appeared at her side. He was slim, with dark brown hair and smooth almond-shaped brown eyes. He had a rakish look on his face, and a slight stubble darkened his jaw.

"Excuse me, mademoiselle," he said, smiling shyly. A distinguished-looking older gentleman was standing by the guy's side, and Jessica glanced at him. He gave her a slight bow.

"You speak English!" Jessica exclaimed, beaming. She quickly dropped all her bags and stretched out her shoulders.

"But of course!" responded the young man with a very sexy French accent.

Jessica breathed a sigh of relief. "Can you tell me how to say *cart* in French?" she asked.

The older man's brow furrowed quizzically. "Cart?" he repeated.

Jessica made a gesture with her arms, pretending to load her bags onto a cart and push it.

"Ah!" said the older gentleman with a charming smile. "She wants *un chariot.*"

"But you do not need a *chariot!*" interrupted the young guy. He put out a gallant arm and picked up her bags. "Would you allow me to be your *chariot?*"

Jessica stared into his warm brown eyes, feeling as if she were going to melt in the liquid fire of his gaze. "Thanks, that would be great," she said gratefully.

Elizabeth stowed her bags on the overhead compartment of the train and glared at Jessica. "I can't believe you handed over your luggage to a complete stranger," she hissed sharply.

Jessica smiled innocently. "What's the problem? I thought it was very nice of him to help me out— especially when my own sister wouldn't," she added pointedly.

Elizabeth shook her head. Somehow Jessica managed to turn everything around. It wasn't *her* fault that Jessica insisted on bringing her entire wardrobe with her. Elizabeth was doing her a favor by coming with her on this trip in the first place. She shouldn't have to be her porter as well.

"Besides, he happened to be gorgeous," Jessica added with a grin.

Elizabeth clenched her jaw. Sometimes her sister's logic was mind-boggling. "You know, thieves can be just as gorgeous as anyone else," she pointed out. "What would you have done if he'd taken off with your luggage?"

Jessica laughed. "Well, I would have had a lot easier time carrying my bags."

Elizabeth rolled her eyes. "Very cute."

"Look, Liz, chill out," Jessica replied smoothly. "He didn't take my stuff, so what's the big deal?"

Elizabeth continued to grumble to herself as she and Jessica took their seats. True, the guy had carried her sister's luggage onto the train. But she was furious that Jessica had taken such a big risk in trusting him. After all, they'd come to France to take care of young children. Jessica certainly wasn't showing a high level of responsibility and maturity.

I have a feeling I'm going to have to keep my eye on her this summer, Elizabeth realized. *Otherwise we'll both end up in a heap of trouble.*

Elizabeth settled into her seat by the window and took in her surroundings. The train was sleek and modern, with lots of legroom and wide aisles. The beige seats were set up in groups of four, with wooden tables between them. Flashing red signs indicated the lavatories and a dining car.

Suddenly Elizabeth felt Jessica nudging her. "Hey, Liz, look who's coming," Jessica said with a wicked grin.

Elizabeth followed her gaze to see the older man and the guy who had helped Jessica making their way down the aisle. "I hope they don't hijack the train," Jessica whispered to her sister.

"Very funny," Elizabeth said, but this time she couldn't help smiling. *Maybe I did overreact a little bit,* she admitted to herself. After all, nothing had happened. She was just in a bad mood because she hadn't gotten any sleep.

"Are these seats free?" asked the older man.

"Of course," Jessica replied graciously, giving him a charming smile.

The younger man took the older man's luggage and stowed it above them. Then they settled down in the seats across from the twins.

"We meet again, mademoiselle," the younger one said to Jessica. "What an unexpected pleasure!"

He kissed her hand, and Jessica blushed in delight. Elizabeth narrowed her eyes in suspicion. The guy might have helped her sister out, but Elizabeth instinctively didn't trust him. He was too smooth for her liking.

"But, but! *Sacrebleu!*" the elderly man exclaimed.

He was gazing at them with a look of surprise. "You are *jumelles!*"

"*Jumelles?*" Jessica whispered to Elizabeth.

"Twins," Elizabeth supplied.

"*Quelle beauté extraordinaire!*" the man exclaimed in wonder. "Such beauty and freshness one might expect to find in a single rose. But in two flowers, it is unheard of!" He waved his hands around excitedly. "Never have I experienced such unique and matching loveliness."

Jessica giggled in delight. His flattery was so outrageous that even Elizabeth couldn't help chuckling.

The man bowed low. "Allow me to introduce myself. I am Louis Landeau, the duke of Norveaux. And this is my son and heir, Jacques," he added.

Jessica's eyes widened. Obviously she was very impressed. Elizabeth shook her head. She hoped her sister wouldn't spend the summer falling all over herself every time she met somebody with a title.

Jessica leaned forward eagerly. "I'm Jessica Wakefield," she said with a bright smile. "And this is my *jumelle* sister, Elizabeth."

"Charmed," the young man said, gazing into Jessica's eyes.

Elizabeth rolled her eyes and looked out the window. *Where's Norveaux?* she wondered, trying to place the area. She quickly went over her French geography in her mind. Forming a mental map, she pictured the country of France and its various regions. There was Normandy in the north, and Bretagne in the west, the Loire Valley in the center. . . . But she couldn't visualize Norveaux.

Elizabeth turned back to the Landeaux. "Where exactly is—"

Her words were interrupted by a loud commotion in the next car.

Suddenly a hefty, red-haired woman came charging down the aisle. She was shrieking in French at a harried-looking conductor, who was bowing and apologizing meekly.

Elizabeth turned her attention to the exchange with interest. At last people were speaking French. Elizabeth squinted in concentration, trying to make out the words. To her delight, she found she was able to understand most of what was being said.

The woman stood up straight. "I am the Countess Doloria di Rimini," she announced haughtily. Her thick red hair was swept up on top of her head, and her cold green eyes glittered darkly, reflecting the chain of emeralds she wore around her fleshy neck. Her pale face was carefully made up, and her jowls sagged. She lifted her chin, as if expecting everyone in the vicinity to bow down in worship.

A tall girl came up behind her. She had a pointy, angular face and luminous green eyes, which contrasted with her short fiery hair. Elizabeth figured she must be the woman's daughter. They looked a lot alike, right down to the grumpy scowls on their faces.

"I demand that you correct this mistake," the woman barked. "My daughter, Antonia, and I should be in first class."

The conductor bowed his head. "I am so sorry, madame," he responded politely in French. "Please accept our greatest apologies. There appears to have been a mix-up. Er, hmmm . . ." His voice wandered off.

"Well, fix it," the countess demanded in an imperial tone. *"Now."*

The conductor seemed to shrink in her presence. "I'm afraid there are no more available seats in first class. Perhaps you'd care to wait for a later train," he sputtered.

"I will not be put off this train," the countess raged.

"Madame, what do you suggest I do?" the conductor asked with a sigh. He was clearly getting fed up with the woman's histrionic display.

The countess's imposing chest heaved. "I suggest that you and your *incompetent* coworkers remedy this *outlandish* situation immediately," she said in a low voice.

The conductor's eyes flashed at the insult. "Countess di Rimini, if you care to enjoy our service, then I am afraid you have no choice but to ride second class," he said. With that he turned and walked away.

"Humph!" the woman exclaimed, sitting down in a huff. "Of all things!"

Her daughter sat down next to her. "Humph!" she echoed.

Elizabeth shook her head. *I can't believe people like this exist!* she thought.

Chapter 4

Eighteen-year-old Prince Laurent paced back and forth across the ornate parlor of his family's château on the coast of France on Sunday afternoon, searching for the right words to say. His footsteps across the marble floor echoed lightly in the airy room. He had called a family conference this morning, and now his father and his stepmother were sitting on the eighteenth-century red velvet divan, watching him expectantly.

Prince Laurent looked at them warily. His father, Nicolas de Sainte-Marie, sat straight on the sofa, his dignified face wrinkled in concern. Catherine, his beautiful stepmother, wore a kind expression on her face as well. They were waiting patiently to hear him out. All he could hear was the crackling flames coming from the stone fireplace.

Prince Laurent groaned inwardly. It would be

easier if his father and stepmother weren't so considerate. The last thing in the world he wanted to do was insult them. But somehow he had to make them understand his point of view.

Finally he faced them, his hands spread wide open. "Well, the long and short of the matter is—I feel trapped," he declared in French.

His father nodded, slowly absorbing his words. "That's not unusual," he responded, speaking in the same cultured French as his son. "Every young man your age goes through this phase."

Laurent winced, biting back a sharp retort. This wasn't just some "adolescent phase" that he would grow out of in a few years. This was his *life*, and he was serious about it. "I don't believe it's just a phase," he said quietly.

His father's deep gray eyes twinkled wisely. He stood up to his full length and clapped Laurent on the shoulder. "Believe me, Laurent, I went through the same thing when I was your age."

"You did?" Laurent asked in surprise. He had never heard anything about this before.

His father nodded. "When I was eighteen, I was a bit of a renegade."

Laurent looked at the refined prince in amazement. He took in his father's silver gray hair, his distinguished bearing, his French-cut royal blue suit, his gold tie clip. His father—a renegade? "What—?" Laurent murmured.

"I think you've shocked him, Nicolas," his

stepmother said with a smile. She lifted up the silver teapot and refilled her china cup. Then she took a sip of tea and crossed her legs at the ankle, her wine-colored raw silk dress rustling. "When it was your father's time to take the throne, he refused it categorically," she said, a glimmer in her dark brown eyes.

At this Laurent sat hard down in a straight-backed gold-embroidered chair. His father had refused the throne? Was the world turning upside down?

His father chuckled. "Oh, they were just boyhood dreams—you know, everybody's fantasy of revolution and equality." He waved a dismissive hand and picked up his pipe.

Laurent sat up straight. "So what did you do?" he breathed, fascinated. He had never really considered his father a role model. Certainly he was noble and dignified, but Laurent had always found him a bit too conservative. But now his father was revealing a side of himself that Laurent had never known about. Or had dreamed could be possible.

His father leaned back on the divan and lit his pipe. "Oh, nothing much," he said modestly, taking a puff.

The princess rolled her eyes. "I'll tell you what he did," she said, leaning forward. "First he refused his title and created a big scandal," she said.

Laurent's eyes almost popped out of his head.

"Yes, and I organized, hmm, a bit of a revolution among the youth of the area," his father added. He smiled at the princess warmly. "Catherine and I were just friends at the time. And she was an active member of our youth group."

The princess stood up and crossed the marble floor. "You have to realize, this was in the seventies," she explained. "It was sort of the thing to do."

For a moment Laurent was speechless. Suddenly the past was being radically rewritten. "And what did grandfather do?" he asked.

His father chuckled. "Nothing. He did absolutely nothing. He told me to go right ahead and make a revolution."

Laurent sat forward eagerly. "And?"

His father shrugged and sat back in the divan, crossing one leg comfortably over the other. "And it was a complete failure," he said with an elegant wave of his hand. "We ended up with the same sort of unjust system as we'd had before, except that it was even more chaotic and less functional."

Catherine laughed softly. "Ah, the follies of youth."

"And so," concluded his father, "eventually I took my rightful place as the head of our principality."

"And married Marianne—your mother," Catherine added.

Laurent was silent for a moment. He stared into the flickering flames of the fire, deep in thought. Somehow he'd thought he was the first in his lineage to question the royal family, to fight against tradition. Maybe his father was more complicated than he'd realized. And maybe there was more to their traditions than Laurent understood.

Laurent turned back to his father. "Why didn't you ever tell me this before?" he asked softly.

His father smiled. "Because it's up to you to fight your own battles and make your own decisions. As the saying goes, the only real teacher is experience. You must forge your own path."

Laurent held his breath. Was his father giving him permission to go off on his own, to construct his own life outside of the royal family? Was his father actually giving him his blessing?

"But I know you will come to value your place in society and take up the responsibilities into which you were born," his father concluded, sounding like his old conservative self.

Laurent let out his breath in a rush. He stood up and walked to the window. Brushing back the heavy velvet curtains, he gazed out at the acres of open meadows. He wished for the millionth time that he hadn't been born into royalty. He was sick of hearing about his family obligations.

Laurent turned and faced his father and stepmother. "I *do* value our family traditions," he said. "It's just that I want my life to be my own."

Laurent's father stood and put a solid hand on his son's shoulder. "Give it time, son," he said. "Think about it."

The kindness in his dad's voice made Laurent feel even worse. *I can't put off my decision much longer,* he realized. But there didn't seem to be any way to compromise. He had to decide whether to sacrifice his own freedom to the royal family or break out and make a life for himself. He had the choice between hurting himself—or hurting his father. And destroying a long legacy of tradition and honor as well.

Laurent bit his lip as he stared out at the endless stretch of land. It was an impossible choice.

"So we all decided to play a prank on the head schoolmistress and transport her *lit*, that is to say, her bed, into the main cafeteria," Jacques was saying.

The train was rolling along at a comfortable pace, and Jacques was telling Jessica a story about his early years at a boarding school in England. His father was sitting next to him, listening with an amused smile on his face. Elizabeth was curled up by the window at Jessica's side, engrossed in her baby-sitting book.

"You know how the English are," Jacques continued. "Boring and—how do you say—*stoufy?*"

"Stuffy," Jessica supplied with a grin.

"Right, stuffy. Well, obviously she was not very pleased. She found out I was one of the leaders and called me to the front of the cafeteria. She demanded that I return her bed immediately." Jacques pursed his lips and imitated the cultured English accent of his schoolmistress. "Mister Landeau, this is an outrage! Please restore the furniture at once! At once!" A small smile curled on

Jacques's lips. "Then she dumped a bowl of hot oatmeal right on my head."

Jessica burst out laughing. "Is that really true?" she asked.

Jacques nodded, a sheepish expression on his face. "I'm afraid so."

Louis shook his head. "Tsk, tsk," he said, chiding his son jokingly. "Jacques, that is no way to win the heart of a beautiful girl. You have to tell her stories of heroic deeds, not of embarrassing moments when you ended up with porridge on your head."

Jacques smacked his palm against his forehead. "You're right! What was I thinking?" He leaned in close to Jessica, his brown eyes dancing with laughter. "Actually, I was just being modest. What really happened is that no one had any food to eat due to a—" Jacques paused, searching for the word. "Due to a strike! Yes, a food strike! So I went off all alone to the next town in search of food. I had to walk for many days and many nights. Finally I found an old farmhouse and brought back buckets and buckets of porridge." Jacques smiled a self-satisfied smile. "And everybody was saved from starvation."

The new version of the tale made Jessica laugh even harder.

"It's no use," Louis declared, throwing his arms up in the air. "It's too late."

Jacques raised his eyebrows. "Is that true, Jessica?" he asked. "Have I totally ruined my chances to impress you?"

"Well . . . ," Jessica teased.

Jacques clutched at his heart dramatically.

"Not yet," she admitted.

"Phew!" Jacques exhaled deeply. *"Quel bonheur!"*

Jessica smiled at his exaggerated expression of happiness, and then they both cracked up.

"OK, enough of this fooling around," Louis said sternly, whipping out a deck of cards. "It is time for some serious business." He shuffled the cards expertly and tapped the deck on the table between them.

"Vous voulez jouer aux cartes?" Jessica asked, repeating the French sentence she had heard at the train station.

Jacques stared at her admiringly. "You can speak French as well!"

Jessica grinned. "Well, actually, that's about the only sentence I know."

"What?" Louis exclaimed. *"You* are modest as well?" He shook his head disapprovingly. "Both of you could use some lessons in seduction. I have had enough of this self-deprecating humor." He gave Jacques and Jessica a stern look. "Is that clear?" Jacques and Jessica both nodded, giggling.

"Good! Now watch carefully," Louis commanded. He fanned out the cards and held them up. "Pick a card."

Jessica reached for a card and glanced at it. It was the queen of hearts. "Now put it back in the deck," Louis ordered.

Jessica did as she was told, and Louis shuffled

the deck again. Then he spread out the cards on the table and told her to find the card. Jessica looked through all of them, but the queen of hearts was gone. "It's not there," she said.

"What?" Louis exclaimed in mock horror. "Not there?" He turned to his son. "Jacques, have you seen it?"

Jacques shook his head solemnly. But then Louis reached into Jacques's shirtsleeve and pulled out the card. "Tut, tut, tut," he said disapprovingly. "Jacques, I'm ashamed of you. What in the world are you trying to pull? Are you trying to steal her heart?"

Jacques nodded.

"Aha!" Louis said. "I thought so!" He gave Jessica a knowing wink. "Watch out for him. He's a foxy one."

A warm glow came over Jessica. Even though it was clear that Louis and Jacques had played this trick before, Jessica found them absolutely charming. She loved Jacques's French accent and the way his brown eyes twinkled with humor. It didn't hurt that he was also a duke-to-be.

Jacques smiled at her warmly, and an electric current raced down her spine. Jessica sighed contentedly. She had been sure this trip was going to be fantastic. And she had been absolutely right.

Is it really possible? she wondered. *My first day in France and already I seem to be falling in love. . . .*

❖   ❖   ❖

As the train continued to speed toward the coast Elizabeth fidgeted in her seat. She was getting bored and restless. She stared out the window listlessly. Miles and miles of beautiful countryside stretched out before her, and the land was getting greener and hillier as they headed toward the South of France. It was beautiful, but Elizabeth's mood was so bleak, she might as well have been staring out at a barren gray landscape.

Elizabeth shifted in her seat and turned back to her book. She stared down at the page, trying to concentrate. *"Time-outs and loss of privileges are effective punishments, but the most efficient method of shaping a youngster's behavior is through the use of positive reinforcement— rewards, such as . . ."*

Elizabeth stopped reading and yawned. She realized she'd gone over the same passage three times already.

She put *The Baby-sitter's Guide* away and pulled out a novel by George Sand, called *La Petite Fadette.* Elizabeth had decided to read only French literature this summer, and George Sand was a heroic figure for her. She had been a feminist before her time. She had used a male pseudonym in order to get her writing published, and she had been one of the first women to wear pants in public. Elizabeth had always wanted to read her novels.

Elizabeth curled up in her seat and read the jacket copy. The story took place in *le Berry,* a small agricultural village in France. It was about an unattractive girl with a great mind and a spirit of independence. Elizabeth closed her eyes and tried to imagine the scene. She pictured rural France and a young, spirited girl. Then she turned back to the book and opened to the first page. But after she'd read a few lines, her mind started to wander again.

Elizabeth dropped the book in her lap and turned her attention to Jessica and Jacques's conversation. The two of them had been talking and laughing for hours.

"Well, he dumped an ice cream shake on me, not a bowl of porridge," Jessica was saying.

Jacques chuckled softly. "It was, how do you say, a sticky situation?"

Jessica laughed appreciatively. "Exactly!" she agreed.

"What are you guys talking about?" Elizabeth asked.

"Heroic deeds," Jessica said. At that, both Jacques and Jessica burst out laughing.

"Huh?" Elizabeth asked.

But Jessica just waved a hand in the air. "It's a long story," she said.

"And not a pretty one," Jacques added, a twinkle in his eye.

I know when three's a crowd, Elizabeth told herself silently, looking around for better company. Jacques's father was napping soundly. In the seats across the aisle the Countess di Rimini and her daughter still seemed to be sulking. The countess was knitting a piece of dark blue wool rapidly, a scowl on her face. Her daughter was staring out the window, a bored pout on her vapid features.

Elizabeth fished through her shoulder bag for something else to read. But she hadn't packed any more books in her carry-on luggage. All she had was a couple of magazines and a box of cream-colored stationery. Elizabeth pulled out the stationery, deciding to write a letter to Enid and Maria. But as she lifted the lid, what she saw made her suck in her breath. Sitting on top of the paper were several envelopes preaddressed to Todd.

A painful lump formed in her throat. *While I was getting organized to write to Todd every day, he was probably planning to dump me!* she thought in indignation.

Elizabeth ripped up the envelopes viciously and stuffed the pieces into the trash receptacle. *There!* she said to herself in satisfaction, wiping off her hands. *I'm rid of him forever!*

But despite her angry gesture, she couldn't help feeling an overwhelming sense of loss. *I wonder what Todd's doing right now?* Elizabeth thought. *I wonder what he's thinking. . . . Is he thinking about me?*

Elizabeth, stop it! she commanded herself. She looked around desperately for a distraction. Somehow she had to keep herself from thinking about Todd. But she was sick of reading, and now she didn't feel like writing any letters.

Elizabeth stood up and inched pass Jessica, who didn't even seem to be aware of her presence. Jacques was regaling Jessica with another story, and she was giggling happily.

Once in the aisle Elizabeth rubbed her eyes and stretched her arms above her head. Her stomach growled, and she decided to get something to eat. She walked down the aisle and headed for the dining car.

After pushing through the last set of double doors leading to the dining car, Elizabeth was surprised to find the car fashioned like a real restaurant. There were white lace curtains on the windows and elegant red tablecloths draped over the tables. A black-tailed waiter hurried about, serving warm meals. The crowd was somewhat raucous. A bunch of young people were sitting at a long wooden table playing poker, and the bar was filled with laughing voices. The rest of the tables were filled with attractive young couples and families. A couple of children were playing on the floor.

Elizabeth headed sadly to the food counter. *Todd would have loved this*, she thought despite herself. She and Todd had always talking about taking a long trip on a train. It was so romantic. She could just see them eating a fancy dinner and laughing as they tried to order in French. . . .

"Vous désirez?" a voice said, asking her what she wanted.

Elizabeth blinked and came out of her reverie.

The older man behind the counter was looking at her expectantly. "Uh," Elizabeth mumbled, scanning the order board on the wall quickly. The menu was written in French, and Elizabeth could only make out a couple of the items. *"Un sandwich au fromage, s'il vous plaît,"* she ordered finally.

"A votre service!" the man replied, reaching for a fresh baguette filled with Gruyère cheese, lettuce, and tomatoes. He handed the sandwich to her with a flourish. *"Vingt francs, s'il vous plaît."*

Elizabeth quickly translated in her head. *Twenty francs—that's about four dollars.* Fortunately the twins had already changed money at the airport. Elizabeth pulled out her purse and dumped the foreign coins into her palm. She fished through the change and picked out two ten-franc pieces.

"Merci!" the man said. *"Et bon appétit,* mademoiselle!"

Elizabeth gave him a small smile and headed back to her seat. She sighed as she threaded through the boisterous crowd. She felt more alone than ever.

On her way back Elizabeth decided to strike up a conversation with the Countess di Rimini and her daughter. *Maybe they're nicer than they seemed at first glance,* Elizabeth thought. *Maybe they were just cranky about the mix-up in their reservations.*

Elizabeth sat down in one of the empty seats

across from the di Riminis and gave them a friendly smile. "So what's your destination?" she asked brightly.

The countess dropped her sewing in her lap and fixed her with a cold glare. "Excuse me?" the woman drawled, responding in English.

Elizabeth swallowed hard. "I was just wondering where you were traveling," she replied lightly. "My sister and I have never been to France before."

"*American*, I presume?" the countess asked, making it sound like an insult.

Elizabeth tried not to feel defensive. "Yes, we're from southern California. We're famous for our lovely beaches, although I've heard the French Riviera is nice. Is that where you're going?" she asked.

The countess snorted. "My daughter and I are traveling on holiday to the summer château of the prince and princess de Sainte-Marie. We will be staying on a small island in the Mediterranean Sea." She stuck her prominent nose in the air. "I'm sure *you've* never heard of it."

Elizabeth took a deep breath and forced herself to let the insult go by. Maybe the countess would take a liking to them when she realized that they were staying in the château too. "That's really a co-incidence!" she exclaimed. "Jessica and I are going to the same place. We're going to be au pair girls for the de Sainte-Maries."

Antonia wrinkled her long nose. "Mother and I don't associate with servants."

Servants! Elizabeth could feel her face burning. She opened her mouth to reply, but Antonia got in the final word. "I would appreciate it if you would stop bothering us. Mummy and I have had a long voyage."

Elizabeth's jaw dropped. *Thank goodness I'm from America—where everyone is equal!* she thought, fuming.

"Excuse me," Elizabeth said quietly, standing up with as much dignity as she could manage. She walked quickly back to her seat, her whole body trembling with anger.

Elizabeth sat down hard in her seat and whipped out her sandwich, taking a furious bite. She only hoped the de Sainte-Maries were more enlightened than these two members of the so-called nobility. A whole summer with a bunch of rich snobs would be pure torture!

Chapter 5

"So what are you doing in France this summer besides stealing men's hearts?" Jacques asked Jessica early Sunday evening.

Jessica made a face, but she blushed despite herself. The train was moving along with a lulling, rocking motion. Most of the passengers were sleeping or reading quietly. Elizabeth and Louis were dozing. But Jacques and Jessica were still up. Jacques had made a trip to the dining car and had returned with beverages, a baguette, and a plate of cheese, along with a bunch of purple grapes.

Now they were sitting across from each other, talking quietly so as not to disturb the other passengers. Jacques was so close that Jessica could smell the faint musky odor of his cologne, and she could practically feel the heat emanating from his body. A delicious tingle crawled down her spine, and she felt her face flushing again.

"Well, you don't have to tell me what you're doing here," Jacques said, a comic look on his face.

Jessica laughed softly, relieved that he had broken the spell. "Elizabeth and I are going to be au pair girls for the de Sainte-Maries," she explained. "We're staying at their summer château." She ripped off a piece of bread and spread some soft Brie cheese on it with a plastic knife.

"Ah! Le Château d'Amour Inconnu!" Jacques said knowingly.

Jessica looked at him in surprise. "You've heard of it?"

Jacques nodded. "But of course!" he said. "It is well-known in France."

Jessica's eyes widened. "Well-known for what?" She took a bite out of her baguette, savoring the taste of the sharp French cheese.

"For tales of passion, what else?" Jacques said with a grin. "*Inconnu* means 'unknown' or 'unheard of.' And of course, the château is known for its strange and mysterious love stories. Its name comes from an old French legend." He reached for the grapes and popped a few in his mouth.

Jessica was enthralled. She pulled her blanket tightly around her shoulders and brought her knees up to her chest, curling up comfortably in her seat. "Tell me the story," she demanded breathlessly.

Jacques gave a half bow with his head. "At your

service, mademoiselle," he said with a rakish grin. Jessica couldn't help giggling.

Jacques put a mock-serious expression on his face and cleared his throat loudly. Then he leaned in close to Jessica, his voice barely a whisper. "Well, supposedly one summer long ago, Prince Frédéric the Third *est tombé amoureux,* that is, fell madly in love with a *jeune* handmaiden of eighteen. Her name was Isadora, and she was sweet and *belle,* with rosebud lips and hair like spun silk."

Jacques paused, and Jessica waited eagerly for him to continue.

"Isadora was just a domestic servant, but she had one extraordinary quality," Jacques recounted softly. "She had a voice of gold. Her voice was pure and sweet like that of a nightingale. When she sang, the canaries sang back. Of course, the union between the prince and Isadora was strictly forbidden."

"So they had a secret affair!" Jessica guessed. She picked up a cluster of grapes and bit off a few.

"That is correct," Jacques said with a nod. He brushed back a lock of hair that had fallen over his forehead. "All summer long they met in secret—in hidden verandas, in the woods, in all the underground passages. . . ."

"There are underground passages?" Jessica breathed, wiping her mouth on a napkin.

Jacques nodded. "What is a castle without an underground passage?" he asked, looking somewhat mischievous. "Now, where was I?"

"The love affair," Jessica reminded him. She picked up her can of lemonade and took a sip through the straw.

"Right, right," Jacques said. "So they had a passionate and tumultuous affair. And all summer long the handmaiden sang as she worked, a pure and beautiful sound that made even the doves sit still and listen."

Jessica held her breath, waiting for him to go on. She felt herself transported back to another world in another time, a magical place of romance and passion.

"But then one day Frédéric was to be wed to a young marquise," Jacques went on. "Torn between his love and his duty, Frédéric agonized day and night. But the preparations proceeded as planned."

Jessica shook her head in disappointment. "Too bad," she said.

"But wait." Jacques held up a hand. "There is more." He picked up his can of mineral water and took a gulp. "On the day of the wedding, which was held outside in the royal gardens, the handmaiden ran into the forest. From deep in the woods came the low, mournful crooning of a sorrowful bird. Tortured by the sound, Frédéric ran out of the chapel and into the woods after her."

"And so they lived happily ever after!" Jessica finished.

"Ah, no!" Jacques said, his face darkening dramatically. "This is a tragedy. Frédéric searched the woods inside and out, but the *belle* Isadora was nowhere to be seen. And so the marriage went through after all. But at the very moment Frédéric took his vows, a beautiful white dove appeared at the altar. It sang a low, sad song, and then it flew away. And it is said that even today on long summer nights, the sweet and sorrowful sound of a mournful dove can be heard."

Jessica sighed. "That's beautiful," she said. "Maybe I'll hear the dove when I'm there."

Jacques winked. "Maybe you will have a mysterious love affair."

Jessica's cheeks flushed at his insinuation.

Suddenly Monsieur Landeau awoke from his nap, mumbling in French. *"Mais qu'est-ce que c'est que ça?"* he grumbled under his breath. *"On est où, là?"* He coughed and muttered to himself. Then he cleared his throat loudly and sat up, glancing around with a disoriented look on his face.

Jacques's expression quickly turned serious. *"Papa, ça va?"* he asked worriedly, trying to find out if his father was all right.

"Eh? Quoi?" Louis muttered, squinting in the dim light.

"Papa? Ça va?" Jacques repeated.

Jessica looked at Louis in concern. Suddenly Monsieur Landeau looked twenty years older than he had before. His tanned face was drained of color and looked lifeless. Jessica wondered if he had some kind of illness. She bit her lip, debating whether or not to call the conductor.

But then Louis seemed to recover his bearings. He blinked a few times and focused on Jacques and Jessica. *"Pas de problème,"* he asserted with a dismissive wave of his hand. He coughed deeply, holding his hand over his chest. Then he drew a handkerchief out of his breast pocket and patted his face.

"Do you want some water?" Jacques asked, quickly filling a plastic cup.

"I'm fine," Louis insisted, the color beginning to return to his face. "Healthier than when I was your age." But he accepted the water gratefully and took a long drink. "The only thing wrong is this seat."

Jacques didn't look convinced, but he didn't say anything.

Suddenly Louis got a playful look on his face. "Mademoiselle Jessica, would you mind trading places with me?" he asked. "I'm an old man, and this seat is terribly uncomfortable."

"Uh, sure," Jessica agreed, standing up quickly.

After Jessica was settled next to Jacques, Louis grinned and winked at his son. Obviously he had just been trying to get Jacques and Jessica together. Jessica giggled at their antics.

"We're French, you see," Louis said with a shrug. "We cannot help it. Romance is in our hearts from the moment of our birth."

Jacques chuckled. "Papa, go back to sleep."

Louis folded up his overcoat like a pillow and

settled into his seat. "But remember, don't do anything I wouldn't do," he added.

"Don't worry," Jacques responded with a smile.

"Prochain arrêt, Marseille!" announced the conductor, walking down the aisle of the train. "Next stop, Marseille! Twenty minutes!"

The overhead lights flashed on, and the train came alive with movement. Passengers started talking and shuffling in their seats. Some of them began gathering their bags and reaching in the overhead bins.

Jacques looked at Jessica sadly. "My father and I are getting off at the next stop," he said.

Jessica felt an unexpected pang of loss. She stared into Jacques's liquid brown eyes, wondering what had come over her. She had just met this guy, and yet she felt as though she'd known him for years. And now she didn't know when she'd see him again. *Maybe he'll come visit me at the château,* she thought hopefully.

Jacques sighed deeply. "I wish I could stay on the train forever," he whispered in her ear. He brushed a feather-light kiss on her cheek, causing Jessica to shiver in delight.

Elizabeth opened her eyes slowly. She was wrapped up in a light brown blanket in the corner, and her blond hair was in a wild disarray. "Hey, are we here?" she mumbled sleepily, turning her head. She jumped with a start as she noticed Louis sitting next to her.

Louis was reading the paper, a cup of coffee in his hand. He grinned at Elizabeth mischievously. "Your sister insisted on sitting next to my son," he explained solemnly.

"Don't believe a word he says," Jessica said with a laugh.

Elizabeth pushed her hair out of her eyes. "Where are we?" she asked again. She pulled her blanket off her lap and began folding it up.

"We're just making a stop," Jessica said. "We've still got a few hours."

"Mmm," Elizabeth said, yawning and stretching her arms over her head. She looked around for a few minutes, watching passengers flurrying around. Then she seemed to get bored. She pulled a book out of her backpack and buried her nose in it.

Jacques squeezed Jessica's hand and tipped his head toward the aisle. "Let's go for a walk, Jessica," he suggested.

Jessica nodded and slipped out of her seat.

As she got up, Elizabeth shot her a stern look. "Where do you think you're going?" she demanded.

"Relax," Jessica told her. "I'll be right back."

"Now, now," Louis admonished Elizabeth gently. "Remember, this is France, my dear," he said. "The country of love."

Jessica giggled at Elizabeth's parting scowl.

Jacques and Jessica walked through the aisles hand in hand, looking for a place where they could be alone. Finally they found a deserted compartment, and they slipped inside.

Jessica stared out the compartment's window. It was twilight outside, making the sleepy French village look enchanted. Tiny pink houses jutted against one another, and the rich Mediterranean Sea glittered a deep blue in the distance.

"It's beautiful," Jessica said wistfully. "Is this where you live?"

"I live where my heart takes me," Jacques said enigmatically. He slipped an arm around her waist and gazed out the window with her. For a moment they stood in silence. Only the low hum of the passengers and the steady movement of the train could be heard.

An announcement for Marseille came over the loudspeaker, and Jessica turned toward Jacques. "You're going to have to go soon," she whispered.

Jacques moved closer, encircling her waist with his arms. Jessica tilted her face upward, wishing he would kiss her.

"Jessica," Jacques said softly. "You're the most fascinating girl I've ever met." He seemed to search in the air for the right words. "You have that certain *je ne sais quoi.*"

Jessica repeated the words to herself silently, feeling a thrill go through her. When Lila had first met Bo, she had talked nonstop about how wonderful and cultured the French were. At the time Jessica had thought Lila was ridiculous. But now

Jessica decided her best friend was right. The French language was incredibly romantic—and so were French men.

But then a wave of disappointment came over her. This was just a brief romantic interlude. She might never see Jacques again.

Jacques brushed back a wisp of hair from Jessica's cheek. "Can I see you again?" he asked, as if he were reading her mind.

Jessica blinked in surprise. "I was just wondering the same thing," she said softly.

Jacques smiled in relief. "I'll come to see you at the château as soon as I can."

Jessica's heart soared. This summer was going to be even more exciting than she had expected. Not only was she going to be living with royalty, but she was going to receive a visit from the son of a duke.

The train slowed down, and people began moving down the aisle.

Jacques coughed and shuffled his feet uncomfortably. "Before I go, I'd like to give you something," he said, pulling a red box out of his pocket. He handed it to her and looked down at the ground.

Jessica took the box and opened it carefully, feeling nervous. Nestled in a midnight blue velvet case was a huge emerald pendant.

Jessica gasped. With shaking fingers she lifted the jewel out of the box, watching it glimmer iridescently in the dim light. "It's beautiful!"

she exclaimed finally. "But . . . but I can't. . . ." She quickly gave it back to him.

"Don't worry, the jewel isn't real," Jacques reassured her. "It's just a great copy." Then he looked at her earnestly. "But even though the stone isn't real, my feelings for you are."

Jessica's heart fluttered wildly.

Jacques pressed the pendant into her hand. "I'd like you to keep it to remember me until we meet again."

Jessica nodded, feeling tears come to her eyes. The sentiment was even more beautiful than the stone.

Then Jacques grinned disarmingly. "But someday I'll replace this fake jewel with the real thing," he assured her.

Jessica shook her head. "It wouldn't have as much meaning as this," she whispered.

"So you did feel something for me as well?" he asked softly, gazing into her eyes.

Jessica nodded.

Jacques put a hand behind her neck and brought his lips to hers, kissing her tenderly. Jessica returned the kiss, and soon they were kissing passionately, like Jessica had never kissed anyone before. Jessica closed her eyes, and the world seemed to melt away. All she could feel was the soft touch of Jacques's lips on hers and the steady beating of his heart. They were locked in a private universe.

But suddenly the train came to a grinding

halt, and Jessica was jolted back to reality.

Jacques touched her softly on the nose. "Until we meet again," he said. He kissed her tenderly one last time, and then he slipped away.

Jessica stayed in the compartment for a moment, savoring the kiss in her mind. She held up the stone to the light, and it glimmered like a secret promise. Jacques was a dream come true. She couldn't wait to see him again.

When Jessica returned to her seat, Jacques and his father were already gone.

Chapter 6

Duty . . . obligation . . . my place in society . . .
Prince Laurent's mind was spinning as he galloped
across his family's property on his white stallion
early Sunday evening. He had been riding madly
for the past few hours, trying to escape from his
troublesome thoughts.

Ever since his talk with his father and stepmother,
Laurent had been racked with anxiety. He had been
replaying the conversation over and over again in his
mind all day, trying to come to a decision.

It's up to you to forge your own path, he heard
his father's wise voice saying. *But I know you will
take up the responsibilities into which you were
born.*

Laurent clacked lightly on the horse's flanks.
"Go, Pardaillan!" he urged him. The horse whinnied and charged forward. A brisk wind whipped

through Laurent's hair, and the lush landscape rushed by in a blur.

Prince Laurent closed his eyes, trying to lose everything in the sensation of the stallion's steady strides. He recalled the wonderful sense of freedom he used to get from riding his horse. His family had come to the château every summer since he was a little boy, and Laurent had spent all his days out in the meadows, riding his horse and practicing his fencing.

Laurent remembered the thrill he used to feel each time he saw the château. With its spiked gables and tall red tower, the old stone castle seemed to be shrouded in mystery. It was the site of courageous deeds and passionate love affairs. The legend of the Château d'Amour Inconnu only added to the mysterious aura surrounding the castle.

Laurent used to ride like wildfire across the fields, dreaming of fashioning his own legend. Alone in the calm of the meadows, he dreamed of meeting a young girl with spun gold hair and the voice of a lark. But unlike Frédéric in the tale, Laurent wouldn't let her fly away.

But now Laurent's innocence was gone. No longer could he enjoy the simplicity of the rich landscape or the beauty of the family legends. His boyhood dreams were only dreams. It was time to face reality.

They reached the end of the meadow, and Laurent pulled Pardaillan's rein, guiding him into the dense forest. The horse slowed down and trotted at a brisk pace along the dirt path.

Laurent stopped near a pond and led his horse to the water. As far as the eye could see were acres and acres of land. The property had been in the de Sainte-Marie family for hundreds of years. Laurent felt overwhelmed with the burden of his heritage.

Laurent sighed. He almost wished that his father had been less understanding. Then Laurent could have gotten angry and self-righteous. It would have been easier to rebel. Now he just felt confused.

As his horse was drinking, Laurent lay down on a soft patch of clover and closed his eyes. He wished he could just stop time right now, that he could put off his decision forever. He envied his younger brother and sisters. They were free—free to live their own lives.

A light breeze caressed his face, and the scent of lilacs wafted in the air. The last rays of the setting sun shone warmly on him. Laurent could feel his tension slowing easing out of his body. He closed his eyes and fell into a deep sleep.

Dressed in his formal royal uniform, Laurent stood at the entrance of a huge ballroom. The music and dancing stopped. Everyone was staring at him as his name was announced.

Laurent walked down the majestic red carpet, and the music started up again. Although he'd attended countless balls like this one, he had a feeling that something was different here. He was supposed to find a treasure here tonight, but he didn't know what it was. . . .

Suddenly his eyes met those of a girl across the room. His heart melted as he watched her. She was absolutely beautiful, with golden hair, ocean blue eyes, and the sweetest smile he'd ever seen. He didn't know who she was, but in his gut he was certain she was The One.

He made his way to her. But just as he was about to put his arms around her and lead her into a dance, someone nudged him aside. And the girl vanished. . . .

Laurent opened his eyes. His horse was standing over him, pressing his nose against the prince's face. "Pardaillan, stop!" He groaned, waving his arms. The horse whinnied softly and nudged him again.

Laurent sat up and sighed in disappointment. The beautiful girl was just a dream.

Jessica gazed out the train window dreamily, her mind whirling with thoughts of Jacques. She missed him already. He was funny and playful, but romantic at the same time. It was an irresistible combination.

The sun was just beginning to set in a luminescent red ball, enveloping the tranquil countryside in a pink haze. They passed through one charming town after another. Small red houses dotted the hills, and sharp white cliffs jutted into sparkling blue waters. In the distance a snow-capped mountain range could be seen.

Jessica gazed in wonder at the extraordinary beauty of the French seaside. Now she understand why the French had their reputation for passion. The South of France was clearly the perfect setting for romance. It was too bad that Jacques wouldn't be at the château with her.

Jessica curled up at the window, dreaming of their next encounter. She hoped Jacques would show up at the château soon. She imagined them frolicking on the beautiful white sand of the Riviera, far away from the countess and her daughter, far away from the little kids. . . .

Jessica glanced at her twin and grinned. *Thank goodness Liz is with me,* she thought. If Jessica were alone, it would be difficult to arrange time off from her baby-sitting duties. But she had complete confidence in her twin. She was sure Elizabeth could handle everything during Jacques's visit.

Jessica closed her eyes and imagined herself and Jacques standing on the shore of the Mediterranean Sea, the wind gently blowing. She could feel Jacques taking her hand. She saw them running across the white sand, hand in hand, stopping only to kiss passionately. . . .

Suddenly the Countess di Rimini started to shriek. Jessica's eyes popped open, her fantasy shattered. The countess was standing in the aisle, shouting in French and gesticulating wildly.

"Mais qu'est-ce qui se passe?" several passengers asked at the same time.

"What's going on?" Jessica asked Elizabeth, whose face was scrunched up in concentration.

Elizabeth raised a finger to her lips. "Shhh! I'm trying to figure it out!" she said.

A conductor rushed to the countess's side. "What seems to be the problem?" he asked.

The countess looked as if she were about to burst. Her face was bright red, and an angry vein popped out of her neck. She was flapping her thick arms around like a bird, and her chest heaved up and down in agitation. *"Mais ce n'est pas possible!"* she screeched. *"Ce n'est pas possible!"*

"What's not possible?" Jessica asked quickly.

Everybody had turned to listen, and a number of passengers from others cars were gathering around to see the commotion.

"J'ai perdu mes bijoux!" the countess was yelling, her voice high and shrill. *"On a volé mes bijoux de famille! C'est un désastre!"* She flung her arms out in a hysterical gesture. *"Quelle horreur!"* Then she swooned dramatically and fell into her seat in a faint.

Antonia shook her quickly. *"Maman, Maman,* wake up!" she said anxiously. She fanned her mother's face quickly. Then she pulled a packet of smelling salts out of her bag and wafted them under her mother's nose.

"Liz! What's going on?" Jessica insisted.

"She says she's been robbed," Elizabeth explained to Jessica quickly. "Her family jewel is missing."

Jessica's eyes lit up. "How exciting!" she breathed.

Elizabeth looked at her as if she were insane.

"OK, make way, everybody! Everybody out!" the conductor ordered in English, trying to clear the aisle. "Everybody back to their seats." Eventually the disappointed crowd dispersed.

The countess quickly regained consciousness. Her eyes popped open, and she waved away the smelling salts. Soon she was up on her feet again, screaming in French.

"Now, ma'am, if you could just calm down," the conductor suggested, biting his lip nervously.

"Calm down! Calm down!" shrieked the countess in English, waving her arms around wildly. "I want the police! Immediately!"

The conductor nodded. "Yes, yes. We're going to contact the local police station as soon as possible."

"I should hope so!" huffed the countess.

"Now, when did you lose the jewel, Madame di Rimini?" the conductor asked.

"Coun-tess!" the countess barked.

The conductor blanched. "Excuse me, Countess."

"That's better." The countess sniffed.

The conductor shifted his feet impatiently. "Please, if you could just cooperate. We need to make a full report."

"Well, how should I know when I lost my

jewel?" she asked self-righteously. "I just noticed the gem was missing. I was checking the contents of my jewel box for a very important ball this evening. This is a family heirloom. . . ." She faced the conductor with a piercing gaze. "Do you understand the gravity of the situation?"

"Yes, Mad—er, Countess, yes, indeed. Now, when was the last time you checked your valuables?" the conductor asked.

"Well, er—," she stumbled. "I believe it was when my daughter and I left Italy."

The conductor looked visibly relieved. "So your jewel could have been stolen at any point along your voyage."

The countess's thin red lips formed a tight line. "Perhaps. But I just know they were taken on this train." Her eyes roamed the passengers' faces suspiciously.

"She's crazy," Jessica whispered to Elizabeth.

"A real nutcase," Elizabeth agreed.

The countess stood up and shook a finger in the air. "I demand that the doors be sealed tight and that every passenger be searched. Immediately!"

The conductor took a deep breath. "Er, madame, I'm afraid that isn't possible. We'd need a search warrant for that kind of thing."

"This is an *outrage!*" the countess shrieked. "Of all the trains I have ridden, I have never experienced such incompetence, such . . ." She seemed to run out of steam and fell in her seat in a huff, gasping for air.

"Shhh, it's OK, Mother," Antonia said, patting her hand.

"Don't worry," the conductor said, rubbing his nose nervously. "We'll do a full investigation."

The conductor circulated in the car, questioning passengers and taking notes. The whole car was buzzing with excitement, and most of the passengers were eager to be interviewed. Finally he got to the twins' seats. "Have you girls noticed anything suspicious?" he asked them.

Both Jessica and Elizabeth shook their heads. "Nothing at all," Jessica said, batting her eyelashes sweetly and innocently at the countess.

The countess pursed her lips, and Jessica smiled to herself.

Jessica was secretly pleased that the countess had been robbed. *Serves her right for being such a snob!* she thought. *I'm sure whoever has the heirloom deserves it a lot more than she does!*

"Finally," Elizabeth said with a groan as the train came to a full stop. She was beginning to think the ride would never end. Elizabeth stood up and stretched. Her whole body ached from sleeping in the chair.

Elizabeth pulled down her suitcase from the overhead bin and fastened her backpack on her back. Jessica joined her in the aisle and reached for her suitcases in the opposite bin.

"Yow!" Jessica exclaimed as she set an avalanche of suitcases in motion. She and Elizabeth quickly jumped out of the way. Jessica's dress bag slid onto the seat, and her three suitcases tumbled down quickly after it. Her duffel bag flew out of the bin and landed in the aisle.

"Jessica! Somebody could have gotten seriously injured!" Elizabeth reprimanded her.

"Not to mention my clothes," Jessica added, yanking out her dress bag from underneath the suitcases. "I hope they're not wrinkled."

Elizabeth shook her head. "Here, let me help you," she said, reaching for a suitcase.

"What?" Jessica asked in mock amazement. "Is my sister actually offering to help?"

"Don't push it," Elizabeth grumbled. She heaved the biggest suitcase off the seat and retrieved Jessica's duffel bag, slinging it over her shoulder. Then she joined the throng of passengers getting off the train.

Jessica squeezed in behind her, struggling with her remaining bags. Elizabeth didn't know how Jessica had managed at all at the airport in Paris. Now she wished she had helped her.

Maybe then she wouldn't have met Jacques Landeau, Elizabeth reflected as she and Jessica got off the train. The guy struck her as being too good to be true. But she knew better than to give Jessica

NOW A HIT TV SERIES!

3 Books FREE Plus 1 More Book For Just 99¢*

FRANCINE PASCAL'S
SWEET VALLEY High.

Experience the ups and downs of being a teenager!

<u>No</u> Risk! <u>No</u> Obligation To Buy! <u>No</u> Commitment!

Here's What You Get:

1. 3 books FREE plus 1 more for just 99¢ plus shipping and handling (and sales tax in NY and NJ). Then, about once a month, you'll get another brand-new SWEET VALLEY HIGH adventure plus three terrific SVH volumes that you can keep for just collection or swap with your friends with no obligation to buy. Keep them and pay our low regular price, currently just $2.99 each (plus shipping and handling, and sales tax in NY and NJ). **That's a savings of 25% off the current cover price!**

2. FREE PREVIEW Each monthly shipment of four books is yours for a 15-day risk-free home trial.

3. FREE BONUS A radical personal Datebook/Organizer **YOURS FREE!**

4. HOT OFF THE PRESS Each new SVH novel will be hot-off-the-press and in your hands weeks before it hits the bookstores.

5. NO OBLIGATION If you're not satisfied, you don't pay a penny! You're never under any obligation to keep the books you receive. If you don't care for one month's shipment, just return the books at the end of the 15-day trial period.

6. OUR EXCLUSIVE GUARANTEE You may drop out of this subscription program at any time. Just write "cancel" on your invoice. Because this is a book service — not a book club — there's no obligation to buy any minimum number of books.

It's all here...first love...best friends...sibling rivalries...the mystery of boys... frustrations with parents...especially FOR TEENS LIKE YOU!

Mail your Order Card & Free Gift Certificate Today!

*Plus shipping and handling (and sales tax in New York and New Jersey). Prices higher in Canada

her opinion. Any sign of opposition would only make Jacques seem more attractive.

But then, Elizabeth thought, *it doesn't really matter.* After all, Jacques and his father were long gone—and the twins would never see them again.

As soon as they were inside the train station both girls dropped their bags on the floor. "Now what?" Jessica asked, rubbing her neck with her hand.

Elizabeth peered at the signs. This train station was much smaller than the last one. There was just one main room and a cute little café with a coffee bar. Elizabeth spotted a sign that said *Sortie* and pointed toward it. "That's the exit," she said. "It must be that way."

"Aye, aye, Chief," Jessica said, bubbling over with good spirits.

Elizabeth picked up the straps of the two suitcases and headed toward the sign. Suddenly Jessica's suitcase wobbled and fell onto its side.

"Hey, what's with this?" Elizabeth asked, picking it up. Then she dropped it quickly, shaking out her wrist. The suitcase felt like it weighed about two tons.

"It's missing a wheel," Jessica explained. "You've got to carry it."

Without giving her sister time to protest, Jessica picked up the straps of her remaining two suitcases and hurried off. "Hurry up, Liz!" she called over her shoulder.

Elizabeth took a deep breath and lifted the

suitcase with a groan. "Hey, Jess, what'd you pack in here? Lead weights?"

"Dumbbells," Jessica answered with a wry smile. Then she waved her sister on. "Liz! C'mon! The royal family is waiting for us!"

Elizabeth shook her head. Suddenly she wasn't so sorry she hadn't helped her sister at the airport in Paris.

Several uniformed drivers were standing near the exit, holding signs with the names of the passengers they were there to meet. Elizabeth scanned the crowd. Finally she caught sight of a sign that said Wakefield. A dignified-looking man in a red uniform was holding the sign.

"Look, Jess! There's our name," Elizabeth pointed out.

Jessica gave a little squeal of excitement, and the girls hurried up to the uniformed chauffeur. He bowed elegantly. "You must be the Wakefield twins," he said in English, a British accent to his voice. "I am Gaston. Delighted to meet you. This way, please." Gaston picked up two of the suitcases and led the twins out of the train station.

Jessica and Elizabeth followed the chauffeur to a light blue van parked at the curb. They stood aside as he loaded their suitcases in the back.

"Hey, look who's here," Jessica whispered in her ear. "The witch and her spawn."

Elizabeth turned to see the countess and her daughter approaching. The countess had her nose pointed up in the air, and Antonia followed behind her in exactly the same manner. A uniformed chauffeur was hurrying after them with their bags.

"Come along, Jeeves!" the countess ordered.

A sleek black stretch limousine was waiting at the curb, and the countess marched up to it. Her head swept the crowd imperiously, but she made no sign of having recognized the twins. "If you please," the chauffeur said, holding open the back door.

"Thank you," the countess responded as she and her daughter slid into the plush interior.

"That's not fair," Jessica pouted. "We should have gotten a limo too."

"What difference does it make?" Elizabeth replied. "A car is a car."

Jessica scowled. "We're already being treated like lowly servants."

Elizabeth watched the limousine drive smoothly away. She just hoped that Jessica was wrong. If everybody at the castle was like the di Riminis, Elizabeth would be on the next plane back to the States.

Chapter 7

Louis and Jacques were seated at an outdoor café overlooking the Mediterranean Sea in Marseille on Sunday evening. The evening was warm and mild, and the blue-gray ocean was calm. A shipyard stood to their right, cluttered with wooden piers and small fishing boats. A few men were still out on the docks, carrying heavy buckets of fish and lugging about huge coils of rope.

Jacques didn't respond. He looked out at the ocean and followed its contour directly south, where Jessica and Elizabeth would be staying. He wondered if they had already arrived. He could just imagine Jessica's reaction to the Château d'Amour Inconnu—she was sure to love it.

Jessica is sort of an enigma, Jacques thought, peering out to sea. *A puzzle.* She was full of energy and vitality but had a strange innocence as well.

She seemed worldly and naive at the same time.

Jacques's heart contracted, and he felt suddenly light-headed. *Is this what it feels like to fall in love?* he wondered.

"Jacques, you better eat up," Louis said. "We've got a long day ahead of us tomorrow."

Jacques blinked and looked up at his father.

"I must say, all that excitement has certainly given me an appetite," Louis said, taking a deep breath of the salty sea air. "Ah, nothing like the South of France to cleanse the soul." He picked up his fork and cut into his omelette with gusto.

Jacques took an obligatory bite of his steak, forcing himself to chew and swallow. The steak was done to perfection, but he didn't have much of an appetite. Every time he thought of Jessica, he felt his stomach turn. Jacques frowned and pushed his french fries around on his plate.

Louis looked at him carefully. "Something is troubling you?" he inquired, his brow furrowed. He wiped off the corner of his mouth with a cloth napkin.

Swallowing hard, Jacques looked up at his father, choosing his words carefully. "I'm not sure we did the right thing," he said finally.

But Louis waved a dismissive hand in the air. "Don't worry, son. It's completely harmless. You'll see. It'll all work out in the end."

Jacques sighed. He had a feeling his father would say that. "I know," he said. "It's just that I would have loved to stay on the train and talk to Jessica."

Louis chuckled. "I don't blame you. She's a lovely girl." Then he leaned forward and lowered his voice. "But you know we had very little choice in the matter," he reminded him. "We had to get off when we did."

Jacques nodded. He knew his father was right. They couldn't have stayed on the train one minute longer.

"Besides," Louis said, laughing, "I have a strong feeling you and Jessica will meet again." He sat back and picked up his glass of white wine, crossing one long leg over the other. "Jacques, my boy, we've outdone ourselves this time." He took a sip of his wine, his cheeks gleaming. "It was a stroke of genius—pure genius."

Jacques tried to laugh, but the laugh caught in his throat. A knot of anxiety twisted in his stomach, and his tongue went dry. Once again he felt he was in over his head. And this time his heart was involved as well. Jessica really meant something to him. He had felt a deep connection to her, unlike anything he'd experienced in the past.

"I'm not sure," Jacques ventured. "We could get the twins in trouble."

But Louis shook his head with assurance. "Not a chance," he said with certainty. "The plan is foolproof."

For once in his life, Jacques wanted to back out. He didn't want to go along with his father. He sighed, his heart heavy. He wished they could undo what they had done.

But when he looked up at his father, he noticed the signs of Louis's weakening health again. Despite his father's jovial air, his eyes were tired and his face was pale with fatigue. *He needs me,* Jacques reminded himself. He couldn't back out now.

"Completely foolproof," his father repeated.

"I know," Jacques replied softly.

Jacques picked up his hot chocolate and stared out at the tranquil sea. If everything went according to his father's plan, he'd see Jessica again. That was for sure.

But it won't be like it was on the train, he thought sadly. *She'll never have the same innocence again.*

"Here we are, girls," Gaston said, steering the car up a long, winding driveway on the de Sainte-Maries' property. They were on a completely private island connected to the mainland by a drawbridge. The property was covered with lush green meadows and tall flowering trees.

Jessica let out an excited squeal from the back of the car.

Elizabeth laughed. "Jess, control yourself," she whispered. "Remember, we're about to meet real royalty."

Gaston pulled the car to a stop at an elaborate wrought-iron gate. Two identical-looking guards in gold uniforms stood at attention in front of the gate.

The chauffeur got out of the car, and the girls followed.

"*Bonjour,* Gaston!" said one of the guards, greeting him politely.

"*Bonjour,* Émile!" Gaston responded.

The other guard opened the back of the car and began unloading the luggage.

Jessica stared at the castle in wonder. It was even more magnificent than she had imagined. It was a beautiful white stone fortress with a moat surrounding it. A number of charcoal gray gables poked out on the left and right, and a huge medieval clock with roman numerals was nestled between them. A tall round, red tower stood in the middle of the castle.

"This is incredible!" Jessica exclaimed.

Elizabeth looked equally impressed. She was staring openmouthed at the sight in front of them. "It's straight out of a fairy tale," she breathed.

"If this is their summer house, I can't imagine how amazing their year-round home is," Jessica whispered to Elizabeth.

Gaston chuckled at their reactions. "Come along, girls," he said to them in English. "You'll have plenty of time to get acquainted with the grounds during your stay." He grabbed a few of their bags, and the guards took the rest.

Jessica and Elizabeth followed them across the lovely grounds. They passed through a tiny gate leading into a well-kept French garden, which was crisscrossed by red cobblestone paths. The scent of lilacs and honeysuckle filled the balmy night air, and birds flew overhead. A tiny footbridge crossed the moat, and they walked across it single file.

Jessica felt her heart rate accelerate as they reached the front door. Long vines of English ivy climbed across the castle walls, and an arch-shaped rose-covered trellis surrounded the entranceway. Gaston unlatched the huge stone door and pushed it open, ushering Jessica and Elizabeth inside.

As they entered the castle Jessica gasped again. They were in a pink marble foyer, which was larger than the Wakefields' living room and dining room combined. Through a big archway to the left was a large salon with a polished floor and mint green velvet furniture. An imposing grand piano stood in the corner, and huge eighteenth-century gold-framed portraits hung on the walls.

Jessica bit her lip in excitement, wondering if this was what Jacques's home was like. *Obviously he and Louis must live in this kind of splendor,* she thought.

Jessica imagined herself as the duchess of Norveaux, residing in a romantic castle like this one in Norveaux. She pictured herself in a long, glittering golden gown, throwing a lavish dinner party for visiting royalty and Hollywood celebrities. And of course, all her friends from Sweet Valley would be invited as well. Lila would be green with envy. . . .

Jessica's daydream was interrupted when an attractive young woman came into the front hall. She was slim, with big, wide-open brown eyes and straight long brown hair tied back in a red satin ribbon. A few dark freckles were scattered across her nose and cheeks.

"You must be the twins!" said the woman in English, giving them a wide, friendly smile. "I'm Anna." She had a low voice and spoke English with just a slight French accent.

"I'm Jessica," Jessica said. "And this is my sister, Elizabeth."

Anna blew a strand of hair off her forehead. "Boy, am I glad to see you!" she exclaimed with a laugh. "These kids are getting to be a handful. Now that they're on summer holiday, they're always afoot." She shook her head and whisked off her apron. "Follow me," she said. "The princess wishes to see you."

Jessica's throat contracted nervously as she and Elizabeth followed Anna down the elegant hall. She hadn't realized that she was nervous about meeting the prince and princess. But the castle was overwhelming and intimidating in its splendor. They passed through a magnificent dining room with a crystal chandelier and an ornate parlor with red velvet divans. All the rooms seemed to have old stone fireplaces in them.

Anna pulled open a door and led them into a small, sunny room with three huge bay windows looking out over the back of the castle. Through the window Jessica could see miles of rolling hills leading up to a dense green forest.

A tall, poised woman was seated at an ornate gilded desk. She looked up as they walked in. "Welcome, girls!" she said warmly, speaking English with a strong French accent. "Welcome to my home." Pushing back her chair, she stood up and walked over to them.

"Princess Catherine, this is Jessica," Anna began, pointing to Elizabeth. But then she furrowed her forehead. "Or are you Elizabeth?"

The girls laughed. "I'm Elizabeth," Elizabeth corrected her. "And this is Jessica."

The princess shook both their hands. "Well, I'm sure we'll be able to tell the difference eventually," she said with a gracious laugh.

Jessica watched the elegant woman in awe. She had never seen someone with so much self-possessed grace. The princess's dark, satiny hair was twisted into a tasteful bun at the nape of her neck, and small diamonds sparkled in her ears. She was wearing a wine-colored silk dress accentuated by a long strand of pearls. When the princess moved, she seemed to glide across the floor. And when she laughed, her voice sounded like the tinkling of a bell.

"Anna will show you to your rooms and explain your duties," the princess told the twins. "And after you've settled in a bit, I'll introduce you to the children. They're eager to meet you." Then she glanced at her watch. "On second thought, it's quite late. Perhaps we should postpone the explanation of your duties until *after* dinner."

"I thought I heard the sounds of young American voices," came a kind voice by the door.

Jessica turned to see a distinguished-looking man with silvery gray hair and a gold tie clip standing by the door. "You must be the au pairs," he said, coming forward to greet them. He spoke English as well, with a less marked accent than his wife. The prince smiled warmly, and tiny laugh lines appeared at the corner of his eyes.

"Jessica and Elizabeth, may I present Prince Nicolas de Sainte-Marie?" the princess asked.

Jessica fought back the urge to curtsy and nodded, unsure how to greet him. She glanced at Elizabeth quickly, but she just shrugged, obviously at a loss as well. The prince seemed to be aware of their confusion and chuckled.

"In France we kiss on both cheeks as a greeting," he said, giving the twins light pecks on the cheeks. Then he winked at them. "And sometimes we give four kisses."

The princess shook her head. "You can't imagine how tiresome the custom becomes when you throw a royal ball!"

The girls laughed, and Jessica felt herself relaxing. The prince and princess were warm and understated. They were nothing like the snobby countess and her daughter.

"Well," the princess said, clapping lightly. "The children will be served dinner in about twenty minutes. After you two have settled in, you may go to the kitchen and join them."

She smiled warmly. "Anna, would you please show the twins to their rooms?"

Anna nodded. "Of course, *Votre Altesse*," she said, employing the French term for "Your Majesty." Then she turned and headed out the door. "Right this way, girls."

Jessica frowned. She had hoped they would eat with the royal family at the regal dinner table that they had passed.

But as she and Elizabeth followed Anna up a long stone staircase, Jessica smiled. *Once the princess realizes that a duke's son is in love with me, I'm sure I'll be accepted as one of the family around here.*

"Imagine all the people who have stayed in this very room over the years," Elizabeth said as she and Jessica settled into their new quarters. She heaved her suitcase up on the bed, sending up a cloud of dust.

Jessica coughed and waved her arms wildly in the air. "I don't think anybody's been here for a long time," she disagreed, making a face.

Elizabeth smiled at her twin's grumbling. The girls had been assigned to two tiny, circular rooms at the top of the stone tower, and Jessica was miserable about it. "But this is the attic!" she had complained. The rooms were light and dusty, with wooden floors and long cracks in the yellowing walls. There were rectangular French windows all around with panoramic views of the island.

Jessica had immediately claimed the larger room, which was equipped with a chest of drawers and a tiny bureau with an antique mirror hanging over it. Elizabeth had happily agreed, preferring the cozy charm of the smaller room. Jessica didn't have a closet in her room, so Elizabeth had offered to share hers.

Elizabeth put her hands on her hips and surveyed the small space. A twin-size four-poster bed with a down quilt was pushed against the wall. An old rickety chest of drawers stood against the opposite wall next to a nonworking fireplace, and an antique cherry desk was in front of the window. In the corner was an old iron washstand with a dusty silver pitcher underneath it.

"This must have been an old *chambre de bonne*," Elizabeth remarked.

"Care to translate?" Jessica asked with a scowl, kneeling on the ground and unzipping her suitcase. She picked it up and turned it upside down, dumping the entire contents on Elizabeth's bed.

"A *chambre de bonne* is a maid's quarters," Elizabeth explained. "In France the domestic staff often lived in small attic rooms."

"Maid's quarters!" Jessica responded in disgust.

She fished through the pile of clothes, separating out skirts and dresses. "I can't believe we're living in a castle and we're staying in a dump," she grumbled. She turned the skeleton key in the latch of the solid oak armoire and pulled out a handful of wire hangers. "Gross!" she exclaimed, wiping dirt off the hangers with the back of her sleeve.

Elizabeth stared at her twin in amazement. "A dump? What are you talking about?" she asked incredulously. "This place is incredible, filled with history and culture. And the view is breathtaking."

Jessica exhaled wearily. "I'd gladly trade all that for some closet space," she complained. "And nicer furniture." She picked up a pile of dresses and began hanging them up in the closet.

Elizabeth shrugged. "It's cozy," she said.

"Which is another way of saying it's a *tiny* dump," Jessica retorted. After hanging up the last of her clothes, she let out a loud *hmmph* and walked out of the room.

Elizabeth shook her head and returned to her unpacking. She thought the room was absolutely perfect. It was old and romantic, with an almost magical feel to it.

Elizabeth imagined herself waking up in the morning with the sun streaming through all the windows. She would push back the lace curtains and gaze out at the extraordinary view. And then she would sit at the beautiful old desk and write in her journal. Elizabeth sighed. She felt like a girl in a fairy tale.

Ever since they had crossed the drawbridge leading to the island, Elizabeth had felt some of her old energy returning to her. It *was* exciting that they were spending the summer on a private island in the South of France. She was sure to learn more about French culture in one summer than she had learned in all her years in Ms. Dalton's class. And her French would improve immensely.

A beam of moonlight peeked through the window, and Elizabeth smiled. *Maybe it wasn't such a bad idea to come here after all,* she thought.

Elizabeth opened her suitcase and lifted out the dresses she had carefully placed on top. She slung them over one arm and opened the door of the armoire. But the closet was crammed full of Jessica's clothes. Elizabeth shook her head. Of course, Jessica hadn't even left her one inch of space. The closet was packed tight with Jessica's summer dresses, miniskirts, and silk T-shirts.

Oh, well, Elizabeth thought, lying out her dresses flat on the bed. *I'll have to negotiate with Jessica later.* For the moment she had to get settled in. Now that she had seen how warm and elegant the prince and princess were, she couldn't wait to meet the rest of the royal family.

Elizabeth hummed as she unpacked the contents of her travel case. She set out her toiletries on the bureau and placed her journal on the marble mantel. Outside, a wind picked up, and a gust of cool air shot through an open window. Elizabeth closed the window quickly, gazing out at the magnificent view. Tiny stars twinkled in the midnight blue sky, and the stormy ocean crashed from afar. The cawing of seagulls could be heard in the distance.

Elizabeth sucked in her breath. She couldn't wait to tell Todd all about the castle and the royal family. But then, words couldn't really capture the beauty of the island. She'd have to take pictures and send them to him.

Then she grabbed onto the mantel, feeling as if she'd been struck. She couldn't tell Todd about the château. She was never going to speak to him again. The sense of loss hit her so hard that she felt out of breath.

Almost against her will, Elizabeth unzipped the inside pocket of her shoulder bag and pulled out Todd's picture. Her hands trembled slightly as she picked up the frame and stared at Todd's familiar face. *Why did I bring this with me?* she reprimanded herself. Tears pooled in her eyes.

Finally Elizabeth wrenched away her gaze and forced herself to tuck the picture into a side pocket of her suitcase. Then she shoved the suitcase underneath the bed, pushing it against the wall with her toe.

I may be a damsel in distress, Elizabeth thought miserably, *but no Prince Charming is going to rescue me.*

As Elizabeth wiped a lone tear from her cheek there was a knock on the door.

Elizabeth blinked quickly and dabbed at her

eyes. She cleared her throat and tried to compose herself. "Come in," she called out, her voice shaky.

Anna poked in her head. "Time to meet the children!" she announced.

Elizabeth forced a smile on her face. Then she took a deep breath and followed Anna out the door.

"Children, I'd like you to meet your new au pairs, Jessica and Elizabeth," Anna said, kneeling down in front of the kids in the huge kitchen of the château.

Six saucerlike brown eyes stared at them solemnly. The children all had curly dark hair and big brown eyes. Manon, the three-year-old, was wearing a tiny pale yellow dress with a matching ribbon in her hair. She was holding on to her older sister's hand tightly. With her long brown curls and pink cheeks, Claudine looked surprisingly mature for a five-year-old. Pierre, the oldest child, was wearing a blue-and-white sailor suit. He stood huddled close to Anna, holding on to her leg.

They're adorable, Jessica thought, giving them a warm smile.

"Bonjour!" Manon piped up.

"Bonjour!" Jessica responded.

"Now, remember," Anna reproached the little girl lightly. "You have to speak English at all times with your new au pairs."

Manon nodded silently, her eyes wide.

Jessica breathed a sigh of relief. She had been a

little bit worried about dealing with the children in a foreign language.

Anna stood up straight and turned to the twins. "Make sure you're very strict about speaking only English with the children," she said. "One of the benefits they will get from your company is the chance to improve their English."

"Don't worry," Jessica reassured her with a grin.

Anna turned back to the kids. "Jessica and Elizabeth came all the way from America to be with you," she said.

Claudine's eyes grew wide. "America!" she breathed.

Anna smiled and patted her on the head.

"Did you take a *bot?*" Pierre ventured.

Jessica giggled. "No, we took a plane."

Pierre jumped up and down excitedly. "Vrroom!" he exclaimed, making a motion of a plane with his hand.

"Exactly!" Elizabeth said.

"OK, children, time for dinner," Anna said, leading the group to the other side of the kitchen. A big, round table covered with a beautiful pale blue tablecloth stood in the corner by a bay window.

"Up you go!" Anna said, lifting Manon into a high chair. The other children scampered to their seats.

They're little angels, Jessica thought in relief as she watched Anna interact with the children. They obeyed Anna just as if she were their own mother.

Anna gestured toward the stove across the

room, where several pots were simmering. "Help yourselves to a meal," she told the twins. "The cook has prepared bouillabaisse and steamed vegetables this evening."

"What's bouillabaisse?" Jessica whispered to Elizabeth as they headed across the enormous room.

"I think it's some kind of fish soup," Elizabeth said.

Jessica wrinkled her nose. "Gross!" she complained. "It's bad enough that we have to have dinner in the kitchen, but we have to eat fish soup as well."

"Doesn't bother me," Elizabeth said, glancing around the airy room. "This could easily be a ballroom."

Jessica had to admit her sister was right. The kitchen was enormous, with a red brick fireplace in the corner and a gigantic old-fashioned stove against the wall. Huge brass pots and pans hung down from hooks on the ceiling.

Jessica lifted the lid of the pot of soup and sniffed it. *It doesn't smell so bad,* she thought, remembering how hungry she was. She filled up two bowls while Elizabeth ladled out steamed vegetables onto their plates. Carrying their bowls of soup carefully, the girls joined the children at the table.

Anna adjusted Manon's bib and stood up. "It looks like you're all set," she said with a smile. "I'll check on you later to make sure everything's okay."

"See you later," Jessica said.

Anna waved and headed out the door.

111

Jessica was totally psyched to get to know the children. When she had been a junior counselor at Camp Echo Mountain, she had been a huge success with her little eight-year-old charges. The kids had adored her and had imitated her every word. At camp she had been solely responsible for eight little girls. Now she only had to worry about three children, and she was sharing the work with Elizabeth. Compared to her junior counselor duties, this job was going to be a snap.

"Hi, kids!" Jessica said, smiling brightly.

Pierre gave her a military salute with his spoon, then burst into giggles. Claudine eyed her warily, a slight pout on her full lips. Manon looked up from her high chair and grinned, food oozing from her teeth.

"*Je n'aime pas le céleri!*" Claudine grumbled, picking up a stalk of cooked celery with her fingers.

Jessica smiled encouragingly at Claudine. "Can you tell me what you just said in English?"

"This!" Claudine whined, hurling the piece of celery at Jessica. "I no like to taste it!"

Jessica recoiled as the stalk hit her in the chest and bounced onto the table. "Why, you little twerp!" she burst out, standing up angrily.

"Whee!" Manon laughed with glee, throwing a handful of peas into the air. The peas scattered in the air and landed all over the floor. Pierre tossed his bread at Claudine, knocking over her glass of milk. Claudine grinned devilishly as she watched the milk trickle across the table.

"Oh, great!" Elizabeth groaned, jumping up and righting the glass. She quickly grabbed some cloth napkins from the table and tried to soak up the milk.

"That's enough!" Jessica commanded, her hands on her hips.

The kids giggled, but they didn't say anything. Claudine looked at the twins innocently as she stabbed a forkful of vegetables. Then she held her fork back like a slingshot and shot them at Pierre. "Ping!" she yelled. Pierre ducked, and a shower of carrots and peas hit the wooden counter behind him. Grinning, Pierre grabbed a stalk of broccoli from his plate and readied his arm to retaliate.

"I said, stop this right now!" Jessica yelled.

Pierre made a face, reluctantly lowering his arm.

"Stop it! Stop it!" Claudine repeated, imitating her.

Well, at least she's speaking English, Jessica thought dryly, scooping up a handful of peas from the floor. Elizabeth returned to the table with a sponge and began wiping up the milk. Jessica quickly cleaned up the vegetables from the table. She headed to the sink and dumped the contents into the garbage can. Elizabeth followed her with a handful of wet napkins.

"I think these little monsters should be sent to bed right now, without finishing dinner," Jessica grumbled.

"Absolutely not," Elizabeth disagreed, wringing out the sponge in the sink.

"Well, do you have a better idea?" Jessica asked, her hands on her hips.

"According to my baby-sitting guide, children should be reasoned with—not punished," Elizabeth explained as they headed back to the table. "They're probably stressed out about meeting us," she added. "This is simply their way of sharing their feelings."

Jessica rolled her eyes and took her seat. Now Manon was banging her hands against her tray and Claudine was building a fort on her plate with her vegetables. Pierre was pretending to drive his beets around the fort. Jessica looked at her plate and realized that she'd lost her appetite.

Elizabeth moved her seat closer to Manon's chair and began a serious conversation with her. "Do you like to play outside? Maybe tomorrow you can show me your favorite place. . . ." She reeled back as Manon shot a handful of warm bouillabaisse into her face.

Just at the moment the kitchen door swung open. "Is everything OK?" Anna asked.

Elizabeth's face reddened, and she quickly wiped the dripping soup from her face. Jessica swallowed hard and looked down. From the way things were going, it looked like she and Elizabeth might not be working at the château for long.

Anna took one look at their horrified faces and laughed. "Don't worry, you'll get the hang of being au pairs in no time," she assured them. "It just takes practice."

Jessica was doubtful. It looked like these kids

would demand more attention than her eight campers combined.

Claudine banged her fork on the table. "I want to see Laurie!"

"Yeah, we want to see Laurie," Manon and Pierre joined in. Soon the three of them were clapping and chanting, "Laurie! Laurie! We want to see Laurie!"

Elizabeth gave Anna an inquiring glance. "Laurie?" she mouthed.

"'Laurie' is Prince Laurent, the children's older brother," Anna explained. "The children adore him."

A prince! Jessica thought excitedly.

"Excuse me, I'm just going to go wash up," Elizabeth said. "I'll be back in a minute." She threw her napkin on the table and hurried out of the kitchen.

Anna began clearing dishes, and Jessica stood up to help her. She stacked up the children's plates and carried them to the sink. "So when will we meet Prince Laurent?" Jessica asked Anna, trying to sound casual.

"I'm not sure about that," Anna said. "You probably won't see much of him while you're here."

Jessica's face fell, but she tried not to let her disappointment show. "Oh?" she asked.

"Prince Laurent is very reclusive," Anna explained. "He spends most of his time alone, reading and thinking." Then she chuckled softly. "Of course, all that might change now that Antonia di Rimini is visiting the château."

"What do you mean?" Jessica asked.

But Anna just shrugged, giving her a pointed look.

Prince Laurent and Antonia? Jessica thought, grimacing. She was totally bummed. A real live prince—and he was a dud.

Thank goodness I already met Jacques! she told herself.

Chapter 8

"Come, children," Anna said, as she pushed back her chair after breakfast on Monday morning. "Elizabeth and Jessica are going to play with you outside today."

Elizabeth took a last sip of her espresso, feeling relaxed after a refreshing night's sleep and a delicious breakfast. Elizabeth had woken to a blue sky and a sun-filled room. When she and Jessica had come downstairs, the table was already set with fresh croissants and bowls of yogurt and granola.

"Shall we clear the dishes?" Claudine asked, sitting straight in her chair. She looked darling in a white lace dress and matching boots. Her hair was pulled up in a thick barrette, and long brown ringlets streamed down her back.

Anna smiled. "That would be lovely."

Elizabeth watched the exchange with suspicion. The children had been startlingly well behaved at

117

breakfast, but Elizabeth had a feeling that this was because of Anna's presence.

Claudine scraped off the dishes and piled up the silverware on top of them. Then she stood up and carefully carried the pile to the sink. Pierre stacked up the breakfast bowls and followed her solemnly.

"I want to play!" whined Manon from her high chair, flailing her little dimpled arms about.

Elizabeth picked her up and swung her high in the air. Manon laughed with glee.

After the table was cleared, Anna led the twins outside. The children followed in a line like little angels.

Elizabeth sucked in her breath as they got outside. It was a beautiful, clear day. Lush green meadows stretched out for miles, meeting up with the dense forest. A sparkling lake could be seen through the trees, and a neat maze of square hedges stood off in the distance to the right. Directly in front of the castle was a wild rose garden, which perfumed the balmy summer air with its sweet scent.

Anna led them past a covered gazebo, where the countess and her daughter were having tea with the prince and princess. A silver teapot stood on a glass table, and china blue cups were set out.

The countess glanced at the twins as they passed and began to gesticulate wildly, speaking loudly in French. The scornfully pronounced words *"les Americaines"* reached Elizabeth's ears, but she couldn't catch anything else.

Oh, well, Elizabeth thought, shrugging. It was just as well that she couldn't hear what the witch was saying about them.

"Hey, is that a maze?" Jessica asked, pointing to the huge labyrinth of trees far to the right.

Anna nodded. "One of the biggest topiary mazes in France."

Elizabeth was enchanted. "Really? How long has it been here?"

"Supposedly it was constructed sometime in the twelfth century as an amusement," Anna responded. Manon jumped in front of her and stretched out her arms. Anna leaned down and picked her up.

"Let's take the kids into the maze!" Jessica suggested.

"No, that is something you absolutely must not do," Anna said, bouncing Manon on her hip. Her voice was stern and solemn. "The maze is more complicated than it looks," she warned. "You can get lost in it for days." Manon squirmed in her arms, and Anna set her down on the ground.

"Oh, come on," Jessica scoffed.

But Anna wasn't fooling around. "People have been known to go in the maze and never come out," she said.

A chill coursed down Elizabeth's spine. For a moment the girls were silent. Then Anna clapped. "Now, let me show you the children's play area."

Anna led the girls to a designated area that was bordered by low hedges. It was a paradise for children, with a deluxe swing set, a sandbox, and a huge wooden dollhouse in the shape of a castle. There was also a small shed full of toys and games.

"Dollhouse!" Manon exclaimed, clapping. She immediately fell onto all fours and crawled into the castle. She peeked at them from a window, her eyes big in her pale face.

"Well, I'll leave you girls for the day," Anna said. "Call me if you have any problems. I'll be with the prince and princess."

"Have a good day, Anna!" Claudine said sweetly. She and Pierre waved as she walked away.

As soon as Anna was out of sight Claudine flew into action. "I no want to play!" she yelled, her face scrunched up in determination. She balled her hands into fists and jumped up and down. Then she grabbed a doll and hurled it at the wall of Manon's castle.

Manon burst into tears and crawled out the back door of the dollhouse. Claudine ran after her and picked her up. Manon pulled at her sister's long curls, and Claudine started screaming. "She pulled my hair!" she wailed.

"OK, you two, break it up," Jessica said, running after the girls.

Pierre looked unconcerned. He was rolling a big plastic ball along the ground. Suddenly he gave it a solid kick with his foot, and it bounced away.

Then he plopped down on the ground and began digging in the dirt.

Elizabeth bit her lip and knelt down by his side, contemplating if this was OK or not. She remembered her book saying that children should be encouraged to play and express themselves freely. *Is this a creative activity?* Elizabeth wondered.

Suddenly Pierre leapt up and took off running.

Elizabeth stood up. "Pierre!" she called. "Stay in the playground."

But Pierre slipped through the hedges and disappeared.

"Pierre!" Elizabeth yelled, running out of the play area into the meadows. Pierre was sprinting across the field with a clear goal in mind. Elizabeth's face fell as she saw where he was headed—right for the gazebo.

"Darn!" Elizabeth muttered, chasing after him. She reached him just as he was hopping up the steps. Elizabeth bit her lip as Pierre dove across the countess's lap. The countess's teacup went flying out of her hand and crashed against the wall, splintering into bits. Warm tea spilled across her lap.

"Oh!" the countess cried in shock. Pierre slid off her lap and ran into the corner. Anna quickly began picking up the broken fragments of the teacup.

Elizabeth shrank back against the door, her face burning.

The countess jumped up, spluttering. The front of her flowing green dress was covered with a huge tea stain smeared with dirt. "Well, of all things!" she burst out in French, futilely rubbing at the stain with a napkin. "This is a brand-new dress, and now it is entirely ruined!" She pursed her lips, shaking her head angrily.

The prince and princess jumped up as well. "My dear, are you all right?" Prince Nicolas asked in French, taking the countess by the arm. "You haven't burned yourself, have you?"

"No, no, I'm fine," the countess responded in a martyred voice. "I've just experienced a slight discomfort, that's all."

"Oh, Countess, please do accept my apologies," Princess Catherine said graciously. She gave Pierre a stern look. "Pierre! What have I told you about staying in the playground?"

Pierre ducked his head and hid between his father's legs.

"You mustn't blame the boy," the countess said, glaring at Elizabeth. "It's not his fault at all. After all, children will be children." She snorted. "Those au pairs are obviously incapable of controlling the children."

Antonia cast Elizabeth a haughty sneer.

Elizabeth bristled with anger. *Who do they think they are?* she thought indignantly.

"Come along," Anna said, putting out a hand to Pierre. He grabbed onto his father's legs, and the prince picked him up with a chuckle. "You're a handful, aren't you?"

Pierre nodded, giggling in delight. When the prince put him down, Pierre ran to Anna. She took him by the hand and led him out of the gazebo. Elizabeth followed quickly, her face still hot with humiliation.

When they reached the play area, Anna gathered the three children together. "Now, remember," she told them, kneeling down to talk to them. "The twins are your baby-sitters now. You're to obey them completely. Is that clear?"

"Yep!" piped up Manon, an innocent look on her face.

Pierre nodded solemnly.

"All right," Anna said, standing up with an indulgent smile. "Now be good, OK?"

"We promise!" Claudine promised.

"I believe them, don't you?" Jessica muttered sarcastically to Elizabeth.

Elizabeth heaved a sigh. This job was turning out to be even worse than she had expected.

I'm definitely not cut out for baby-sitting, Jessica thought as she applied a second coat of crimson nail polish. She was sitting under a luxuriant weeping willow, watching Pierre and Claudine play catch out of the corner of her eye.

She and Elizabeth had tried to get the children to play as a group, but Manon had refused to give up the ball whenever she got hold of it. Then they had decided to teach the kids how to play softball.

123

The twins had found a plastic bat and a whiffle ball in the playroom and had explained the basics of the game. Claudine and Pierre had caught on, but the game was clearly too advanced for Manon. She was only interested in getting the bat in her hand and pounding it on the ground.

Finally Elizabeth had decided to play with Manon alone, leaving Jessica in charge of Pierre and Claudine. Elizabeth and Manon were across the lawn in the sandbox, and it looked like they were playing hide-and-seek. Elizabeth kept building sand dunes and ducking behind them. Manon was throwing fistfuls of sand in the air and squealing with glee.

At first Jessica had protested about being left alone with the two older monsters. After all, it was the twins' first day at the castle, and Jessica wanted to enjoy it. But now she was glad they had been left in her care. Manon was more work than the two of them combined.

Of course, watching the older kids is still work, Jessica thought with a sigh, waving her wet nails in the air. Out of the corner of her eye she could see Princess Catherine and the di Riminis by the in-ground swimming pool.

When Jessica hadn't seen the obnoxious noble pair the night before, she had entertained the hope that they weren't staying in the castle after all. But it turned out that they had attended some royal ball. They had arrived early in the morning, breezing into the castle with all the pomp of a pair of visiting celebrities.

The countess was stretched out on a chaise lounge, a glass of iced tea in her hand. She was wearing some sort of garish red-flowered silk kimono. Her legs were bent at the knees, and her dimpled elbows rested lazily on the arms of the chair. The princess was sitting on a lawn chair next to her, and Anna was setting out a platter of hors d'oeuvres on a small glass side table.

"Mummy, look!" Antonia called in a grating voice from the pool, speaking English with a cultured British accent. She stepped onto the diving board in a sleek white maillot. Jessica scrunched her nose in distaste as Antonia stood poised at the end of the board, obviously trying to draw everybody's attention. "Look what my swimming instructor taught me!"

"Go on, dear!" the countess cooed, responding in English as well.

Antonia held her arms above her head and dove into the air like a graceful swan. Then she crashed into the water flat on her belly, and Jessica burst out laughing.

Serves the royal snob right, she said to herself.

Antonia surfaced, spluttering. "Humph," she said with a scowl, swimming to the edge. She pulled herself out of the water and shook out her short red hair. "That board is too low," she declared in a petulant voice.

"Remember, dear, we're not at home anymore," the countess said in a comforting tone. "Even the swimming pools here are different."

Jessica shook her head in disgust as Antonia stretched her long white body out on the chaise lounge next to her mother. She had never seen a more spoiled girl in her whole life.

Jessica rolled her eyes and returned to her task at hand. She bent her fingers and inspected her nails. Satisfied with her work, she pulled off her leather sandals and stuck cotton balls in between her toes. Bending over, she carefully applied a coat of polish to her little toe.

"Pierre is throwing *la balle* too hard," Claudine whined suddenly.

"The ball," Jessica automatically corrected her without looking up.

Suddenly Elizabeth let out a shriek, and Jessica gave a start. She nearly spilled her nail polish all over her foot.

Jessica looked up in irritation. "What's wrong?" she grumbled.

"Pierre is running away again!" Elizabeth shouted, pointing across the lawn.

Jessica followed her gaze. Sure enough, Pierre was charging across the meadow as fast as his little legs could carry him. With his arms and legs straight out, he looked like some kind of toy robot.

"Pierre! Come back!" Elizabeth screamed, her hands on her hips. "Pierre! Come back this instant!"

"He doesn't seem to be listening," Jessica pointed out blandly. She wasn't too worried about him. After all, they were on a private island. He couldn't get very far. Jessica leaned down and began carefully painting her big toe.

"I'm going after him!" Elizabeth declared.

Jessica nodded, intent on her handiwork. "Gotcha," she said.

"Jessica, look at me!" Elizabeth commanded.

Jessica glanced up, annoyed. "What is it now?" she asked.

"Don't take your eyes off the girls," Elizabeth warned. Then she strode off after Pierre.

"All right, all right," Jessica muttered, bending down again. Sometimes Elizabeth could be such a pain.

"Pierre!" Elizabeth shouted as she jogged across the enormous expanse of lawn. She caught sight of him hiding behind a big oak tree. "Pierre! I see you!" she yelled, charging after him.

At the sound of her voice he darted out from behind the tree and sprinted across the clearing. Then he slipped into the huge topiary maze.

"Not in there." Elizabeth groaned, watching in dismay as he disappeared into the εnormous tangle of trees.

Anna's warning came back to her, and Elizabeth shivered. *You can get lost in there for days,* she heard Anna's solemn voice saying. *People have been known to go in the maze and never come out. . . .*

Elizabeth put her hands to her head, feeling scared. She had to get Pierre out of there somehow. But Anna would be angry if she found out Elizabeth had disregarded her warning. And what if both she and Pierre disappeared in the twisting labyrinth?

Elizabeth thought quickly. She remembered a passage in her book regarding tone of voice. It had said that children respond instantly to authority. Elizabeth cleared her throat and put on her strictest voice. "Pierre de Sainte-Marie, I demand that you come back here this instant."

She held her breath, but he didn't reappear. All she could hear was the pitter-pattering of his little feet somewhere to the right of her.

"Pierre!" Elizabeth warned, starting to feel slightly hysterical. "If you don't come back this instant, you won't get any lunch!"

She heard him laugh in response. But this time he seemed to be to the left of her. Elizabeth's stomach coiled nervously. He was just a little boy. He could get lost all alone in the maze. Or he could get hurt. *What if he falls down?* Elizabeth worried. *Or what if he gets bitten by a poisonous snake?*

Panicked, Elizabeth rushed headlong into the maze. She found herself in a twisting tunnel of green. The hedges were several feet taller than she was, blocking her view on both sides. The path forked every few feet, and she hurried through it, turning randomly.

Suddenly she stood perfectly still and looked around her. All she saw was a tangle of trees. She was lost already.

"Pierre?" she called, her heart pounding frantically. She heard his laughter and stiffened, listening closely. Elizabeth gritted her teeth in frustration.

The laughter repeated itself, and Elizabeth chased after the sound. But the farther she ran, the more the giggles seemed to change direction. Elizabeth ran left and right along the dirt path. She took turn after turn. But the deeper into the maze she got, the more complicated it seemed to become.

Finally Elizabeth stopped, panting. She looked around, trying to get her bearings. But she was totally disoriented. She had no idea which way was north, and the sound of Pierre's laughter was totally gone.

Don't panic, Elizabeth told herself, trying to stay calm. She'd only been stuck in the maze for several minutes, although it seemed like hours. Obviously there was a way out of the labyrinth. She just had to figure out what it was.

Elizabeth closed her eyes and forced herself to take long, deep breaths. "You need a plan of action," she said to herself. Finally she decided to continue straight ahead, taking only left turns. That had to lead her out eventually.

She walked quickly through the maze, turning

left at every fork. The dirt path was soft underneath her feet, and the hot sun beat down on her back relentlessly. Elizabeth's throat felt parched, and beads of perspiration dripped down her face. But she trudged on with determination.

Suddenly she heard the sound of little footsteps. She stood perfectly still, holding her breath as she gazed around her. The sound of footsteps came again, closer to her.

Elizabeth tiptoed in the direction of the noise, keeping close to the bushes. Then she spied Pierre on his hands and knees, peeking through the hedges.

Elizabeth crept up to him silently, afraid he'd take off again.

"I've got you now," she said, springing on him. She knelt down and held him softly to her, her arm wrapped around his belly. Elizabeth trembled in relief. She would have never forgiven herself if something had happened to him.

Pierre giggled, leaning in closer to her. Elizabeth's anger dissipated immediately. The boy was adorable. "Pierre, you scared me," Elizabeth scolded him softly. "You shouldn't run away like that."

Pierre pressed his finger to his lips. "We mustn't disturb Laurie," he warned her.

Elizabeth peered through the hedges and saw that they were at the edge of a clearing. Obviously they were in the outermost tunnel of the maze. There was a small cottage up ahead. A young man with black hair was fencing with a jousting dummy in front of it. He seemed to be a skilled swordsman.

Elizabeth's entire body flushed at the sight of him, and a strange tingling sensation ran up and down her spine. For a moment Elizabeth felt as if time had stopped. She had the eerie sensation of arriving at the place she had been headed for her whole life.

Pierre grabbed her hand. "Elizabeth, let's go," he said.

But Elizabeth just gazed at the guy, spellbound.

"'Lizabeth!" Pierre repeated.

Elizabeth blinked. "That's your brother?" she asked.

"Yes," Pierre whispered. "But he likes to practice by himself."

Elizabeth silently watched Prince Laurent expertly thrust his sword at the dummy. There was something about him that seemed familiar—his stance, his muscular arms, the chiseled lines of his profile. . . . For some reason he reminded her of someone she knew.

Pierre pulled up a fistful of grass and sprinkled it on Elizabeth's head.

Elizabeth turned to Pierre, the spell broken. Then she shook her head hard and exhaled wearily. "Pi-erre," she said with a groan. "Now stop it!" She quickly wiped the remaining strands of grass from her hair.

Pierre giggled and did a little dance. Elizabeth couldn't help smiling at his antics. She realized that reading books didn't help much when it came to learning to take care of children. Of course, the job would be a lot easier if Jessica would do her share. It was their first day, and Jessica had already managed to let Pierre run off twice.

She'd better shape up immediately, or I'm going to slaughter her, Elizabeth thought.

"Come along, Pierre," she whispered. "Let's see if we can find our way back."

At that, Pierre's eyes lit up. "I know the way easily," he declared. He took Elizabeth's hand firmly in his and tugged her back into the maze.

But Elizabeth felt a strange pull on her heart and turned back to the clearing for a moment. Her breath caught in her throat again as she watched the beautiful guy fencing. He moved as easily and naturally as a wild animal.

I know you, she spoke to him in her mind. *But who are you?*

Prince Laurent leapt into the air and thrust his sword at his imaginary partner. His partner swung his sword forward, and Laurent ducked quickly.

"Attention, *chevalier!*" Laurent yelled, jumping up and lifting his sword in the air. He swiped gracefully at the dummy's sword, his wrist flipping nimbly with each movement. *Click! Clack! Click!*

Suddenly he heard a sound behind him and whirled around quickly. He stood perfectly still, his body coiled. But all he heard was the familiar sound of crickets chirping and birds tweeting high in the trees above him. Laurent shrugged and turned back to the dummy.

But then a dove cooed from a tree branch and flew past him, diverting his thoughts again. Laurent stopped in midair, his sword uplifted. As he followed the path of the lovely white bird, the famous legend of the Château d'Amour Inconnu came back to him.

Every time he heard the sweet sound of a dove, he couldn't help thinking of the romantic tale of Frédéric the Third and Isadora the handmaiden. And he couldn't help dreaming of meeting his *own* fair-haired girl with a voice of gold someday.

Something rustled from the maze again. His sword in hand, Laurent turned quickly to the hedges. Then he sucked in his breath.

A vision appeared through the thick bushes—an angelic girl with golden blond hair and startling blue-green eyes. She was peeking through the hedges, and she seemed to be watching him. Enchanted, Laurent moved forward toward the maze.

For a moment their eyes met, and Laurent's breath caught in his throat. A liquid current seemed to unite them, and Laurent followed it slowly toward her. Time seemed suspended in the magic of the moment.

But then she disappeared.

Laurent blinked and stared at the hedges. "Was

she really there?" he whispered. There was no trace of her now.

Laurent shook his head and laughed at himself. *Now I'm dreaming awake as well as asleep.*

"OK, now it's Manon's turn," Jessica announced. She was playing hopscotch with the girls on the playground. They had drawn the borders of the game in blue chalk on the ground, and Manon stood on the home square.

Jessica placed a pebble in Manon's hand and helped her toss it onto the first square. Manon squealed with delight as the pebble landed in the middle of the square. She jumped up and down and clapped her plump little hands.

"OK, go get it," Jessica said. Manon did a two-legged jump with an extra bounce in between. Jessica giggled at her creative version of the move.

"I got it!" Manon exclaimed happily. She went to pick it up and lost her balance. Jessica grabbed her quickly and steadied her. Then she guided Manon's hand to help her pick up her rock.

"Here comes Mademoiselle Elizabeth *avec* Pierre," Claudine announced.

"English, Claudine," Jessica murmured.

"*Wiz* Pierre," Claudine corrected herself.

"Very good!" Jessica said. Claudine smiled proudly, flipping her curls over her shoulder.

Jessica looked up as Elizabeth approached. She was holding Pierre by the hand, and he was running

134

along happily beside her. As soon as they reached the playground Pierre flew across the ground and dove into the sandbox.

"Pierre, promise me you'll stay put for a while?" Elizabeth asked, eyeing him warily.

Pierre nodded, already engrossed in his new activity. He was on his hands and knees in the sand, drawing circles with a little stick.

"I want to play in the sand!" Claudine shouted. She pulled off her white boots and jumped into the sandbox with him.

"Me too!" chimed in Manon, slipping out of Jessica's arms and waddling after her sister. She promptly plopped down on her bottom, her legs stretched straight out. She dug her palms in the sand and flung handfuls of it into the air.

Pierre chucked his stick aside and flopped onto his back in the sand. "I'm making *un ange de neige!*" he said proudly, gliding his arms and legs back and forth to form the shape of an angel.

Claudine knelt down by his side. "A snow angel," she corrected him pertly.

"A sand angel!" Pierre yelled out. They both giggled.

Jessica sat down on a bench, relaxing for the first time in an hour. It looked like the kids were going to entertain themselves for a while.

"Did you two have a nice walk?" Jessica asked, turning toward her sister.

"Jessica, I've had it with you!" Elizabeth raged.

"I'm not going to put up with your selfish, lazy attitude this summer!"

Jessica reeled back, shocked. She had been playing all alone with the girls for the past hour while Elizabeth was off running around in the maze. And for the first time since they'd been there, the children were actually behaving. *Who does Elizabeth think she is?* she fumed.

Jessica stood up angrily. "Just because I'm not tripping over myself trying to be Miss Perfect all the time doesn't mean I'm lazy," she responded.

"Yes, it does!" Elizabeth retorted. "If you had been doing your job, then Pierre wouldn't have run off again."

Jessica tossed her hair. It wasn't *her* fault that Pierre had decided to run away. And besides, nothing had happened to him. "Oh, Liz, you're such a worrywart," she said in disgust.

"And you're such a prima donna!" Elizabeth returned.

"Well, at least *I'm* not the most boring au pair in the history of the world," Jessica shot back. "Maybe the kids would listen to you if you'd be a little more fun."

"*Fun?*" Elizabeth responded, her eyes flashing. "It's easy to have fun when you're totally irresponsible. I'm sick of being *your* baby-sitter."

Jessica planted her fists on her hips. "Well, I'm sick of it too! Why don't you leave me alone and stop being so bossy?"

"Me! *Bossy?*" Elizabeth yelped. "Who forced me to come here in the first place?"

"Well, if it weren't for me, you'd never do anything with your life," Jessica said in a huff. "You're the most boring person on this planet!"

Sparks shot from Elizabeth's eyes. "And you're the most selfish, unreliable sister imaginable!"

"Well, if that's the way you feel, why don't you go back home?" Jessica yelled.

"Maybe I will!" Elizabeth replied hotly.

"Good!" Jessica returned. Then she caught a glimpse of Anna out of the corner of her eye. She and the gardener were standing at the edge of the playground, staring at them. The kids were silent from the sandbox, watching the fight with interest.

Jessica turned red and lowered her eyes, her lips pursed.

Elizabeth stared at her feet, her arms folded across her chest.

Then Jessica glanced at her sister, wordlessly establishing a stony truce. Obviously they couldn't continue fighting in front of everybody.

But the truce is only temporary, Jessica thought stubbornly. *I'll never forgive Elizabeth for humiliating me like this.*

Chapter 9

Jessica sat outside on a stone bench in the rose garden on Tuesday afternoon, eating a picnic lunch by herself. It was another beautiful day. The sky was a clear, bright blue, and a light rose-scented breeze wafted through the air. Fernand, the cook, had gone out of his way to prepare a French specialty for Jessica called a *"croque monsieur."* It was the French version of a grilled cheese sandwich.

Jessica took a big bite out of her sandwich, catching some melted cheese on her index finger and licking it off. Despite the delicious lunch and the warm rays of sun beaming down on her shoulders, Jessica's spirits were low. She was still fuming about her fight with Elizabeth the day before.

Jessica couldn't believe the horrible things Elizabeth had said to her. Her sister had accused her of being selfish, lazy, and unreliable. *And* a prima donna! Jessica's face burned at the memory. It was so unfair. She hadn't done a thing to deserve her sister's insults.

In fact, Elizabeth's been nothing but unpleasant ever since we left Sweet Valley, Jessica thought angrily. Her sister was acting as if she were doing Jessica some huge favor by agreeing to spend the summer with her in a castle with royalty in France.

Jessica shook her head. She didn't know why she had wanted Elizabeth to come with her in the first place. Her sister was no fun at all. She was treating their au pair job like it was the most important position in the world, and she was treating Jessica like one of the children. Jessica puffed out her cheeks in frustration. She wished Elizabeth would chill out and relax a little. There was no way Jessica could enjoy their trip if her sister insisted on being the baby-sitting police.

After their fight the girls had barely spoken to each other. They had been virtually silent during dinner, only exchanging words when absolutely necessary. Even the kids had been well behaved at dinner, obviously sobered by the twins' solemn moods.

The evening had been endless. When the kids were finally tucked into bed, Jessica had exploded. "This is impossible!" she had exclaimed. "I can't go on like this!"

"Neither can I!" Elizabeth had agreed hotly.

But neither of them had budged. So finally the girls had agreed to split their duties. That way they would avoid spending more time together than was absolutely necessary and the work would be equally distributed. Jessica had taken the morning shift, and now it was Elizabeth's turn to take care of the children.

Jessica ate the last of her sandwich and wiped the crumbs off her hands. She picked up her orange soda and finished it off as well. Then she crumpled up her napkin and stuffed everything into the paper bag by her side.

Now what? Jessica thought gloomily. It was great that she had a break from the kids, but it wasn't so much fun being alone. She wished Jacques would come and visit her. Now that she and Elizabeth weren't speaking to each other, she wanted to see him more than ever. *I wonder what Jacques is doing right now?* she thought.

Jessica leaned back against the bench and drew her knees up to her chest, realizing that she didn't know anything about him at all. She tore absently at a hole in her faded blue jeans, deep in thought. Jacques looked like he was about her age, so he must be in high school. But she had no idea what a duke's son did over summer vacation. *Maybe he spends the break out on the beach, windsurfing and sailing*, Jessica pondered. *Or maybe he travels to exotic places all over the world with his father.*

Suddenly a white dove flew overhead, crooning softly. Jessica sucked in her breath, reminded of the legend of the Château d'Amour Inconnu. She watched breathlessly as the beautiful bird fluttered around a rosebush. Then the bird let out a plaintive cry and flew away. Jessica exhaled sharply. She was sure it was a sign. Obviously she was meant to have a mysterious romance this summer. Fate had brought her and Jacques together.

Even though she had just seen Jacques two days ago, the train ride seemed like a distant memory now. Jessica closed her eyes, dreamily remembering Jacques's passionate kiss on the train and the intense look in his liquid brown eyes. She could feel his strong arms around her waist, and she could hear his soft voice whispering, *Until we meet again.*

"Mademoiselle, I have mail for you," Anna called, startling Jessica out of her daydream. Jessica open her eyes quickly, blinking in the sun.

Anna was approaching from the castle, waving a letter in her hand. *It must be from Jacques!* Jessica thought excitedly. A letter from home couldn't possibly have reached her so fast. *What a wild coincidence!* she thought. His letter had arrived at the exact moment she was thinking about him. They definitely had a cosmic connection.

"Looks like somebody has an admirer," Anna with a smile, her brown eyes sparkling.

Jessica jumped up, her cheeks flushing happily. "Thanks, Anna!" she said, taking the letter from her outstretched hand.

"My pleasure!" Anna responded with a wink. "I

always like to help out in affairs of the heart." She turned and headed for the gazebo.

As soon as Anna was out of sight Jessica turned the letter over, a small smile on her face. Then she jumped as if she had been burned. The letter was addressed to Elizabeth, and it was from Todd. It had been sent Express Mail. Jessica's heart sank to her feet.

"Express Mail," she grumbled in disgust. "I wonder what Mr. Boring as Toast has to say that's so important."

Jessica tapped the envelope on her palm, thinking of how sad Elizabeth was about Todd. After he had broken up with her for the summer, her sister had cried for about twenty-four hours straight. But now she seemed to be doing better. She hadn't mentioned his name for a few days. *Elizabeth is just starting to get over him,* Jessica told herself. *It's a shame that he's bothering her again.*

Jessica stood up and headed for the playground to deliver the letter. She sighed, feeling sorry for herself. *I'm the one who deserves a love letter,* Jessica thought. *Especially after the way Elizabeth abused me in public yesterday.*

Suddenly she stopped in her tracks. What was she doing, delivering Elizabeth's mail to her? Had she lost her mind? Once again, Elizabeth's mean words came back to her. *You're the most selfish, irresponsible sister imaginable!* she heard Elizabeth's sharp voice yelling. Jessica felt her blood boiling again.

You want to see selfish? Jessica responded in her mind. *Fine!*

Jessica did an about-face and headed directly to the château, stuffing the letter into the back pocket of her jeans. She breezed into the kitchen and dropped her lunch bag in the trash.

"How was your *déjeuner*, Mademoiselle Jessica?" Fernand asked. He was standing at the counter, chopping up fresh vegetables on a cutting board.

"It was *délicieux!*" Jessica responded.

Fernand beamed with pleasure. *"Tant mieux!"* he said. "So much the better!"

Jessica walked casually down the hall and tip-toed into the parlor. A fire was crackling in the hearth as usual, but the room was entirely deserted. Jessica looked around quickly. Then she held her breath, listening for voices. Nobody was in the vicinity.

Her pulse quickening, she pulled the letter out of her pocket. She hesitated for a moment, then she shoved it into the fireplace. The fire crackled loudly and the red flames licked hungrily at the sides of the envelope.

Sweet revenge! Jessica thought. Feeling guilty but happy, Jessica folded her arms and watched the letter disintegrate into nothing.

"Pierre, stop throwing the books," Elizabeth snapped.

Pierre turned to her guiltily, an oversize hardcover

book in his outstretched arm. Pouting, he slowly lowered his hand to his side.

It was late in the afternoon and Elizabeth was in the nursery with the children, trying to read a story to them. The children had a whole bookshelf full of English books, and this was their favorite. It was called *The Big Apple* and recounted the tale of a little French girl who took a trip to New York City. She befriended an elephant that had escaped from the Bronx Zoo and hid out with him in Central Park.

The girls were enthralled with the story. Curled up on either side of Elizabeth, they were taking in her every word. But Pierre wouldn't sit still. He was having more fun pulling books off the shelves and pitching them at the wall. A pile of children's books was already scattered all over the floor.

Where is Jessica? Elizabeth wondered, checking her watch. Her twin should have taken over two hours ago. Sighing, she turned back to the story.

"And so Susanna jumped up on Edward the Elephant's back," Elizabeth read aloud. "He lifted his big trunk in the air, and they galloped through the snowy woods in Central Park together."

"Is that Central Park?" Claudine asked, pointing to the picture.

"There's Edward!" Manon exclaimed.

Another book hit the wall with a loud thud. "That's it! I've had it," Elizabeth declared firmly, slamming the book shut.

"But we're not finished with the story!" Claudine protested.

"Book! More book!" Manon yelled out. She leapt to her feet and jumped up and down on the couch. Picking up a pillow, she flung it at Pierre.

Pierre ducked, and the pillow hit the wall. Pierre danced on his little feet, sticking out his tongue at Manon. Manon started to cry.

Elizabeth felt like pulling out her hair. Standing up, she placed her hands firmly on her hips. "Pierre, I want you to pick up every single book right now," she said in a quiet, authoritative tone.

Pierre looked at her with big round eyes. Then he turned his lips down and began picking up books.

"Claudine, will you please put the pillows back on the couch?" she asked with a sigh.

"OK, Elizabeth," Claudine agreed, obviously sensing her distress.

"And you," Elizabeth said, reaching for Manon and picking her up in the air. "You sit with me." Manon stopped crying and wrapped her arms around Elizabeth's neck. Elizabeth breathed a sigh of relief, sitting down with her on her lap.

Pierre glanced at her through lowered eyelids. "Everything's all cleaned up now, 'Lizabeth," he said.

"Great!" Elizabeth said with a smile. She patted the space by her side. "Now if you'll sit here quietly, I'll let you read out loud."

"I want to read too!" Claudine yelled.

Elizabeth nodded. "You'll both get your chance."

Elizabeth laid the book open on Pierre's lap and indicated where he should pick up with the story.

"All the zookeepers came, and Edward the Elephant hid behind a tree. But he was too big. . . ." Pierre read.

Elizabeth glanced at her watch again. She couldn't believe the audacity of her twin. Yesterday Jessica had spent the morning painting her nails instead of watching the kids, and today she wasn't even bothering to show up.

"What's a 'sleigh ride'?" Pierre asked, pointing to the page.

"It's a ride in the snow on *un traîneau,* a sled," Elizabeth explained.

Just then the door opened and Jessica breezed in, smiling. "Are we ready to have some real fun, kids?"

Manon hopped off Elizabeth's lap and ran to her sister. "Jessica! Can we go swimming again?" She held out her arms and Jessica picked her up, giving Elizabeth a triumphant smile.

Elizabeth glared at her sister. She was about to give her a piece of her mind, but then she bit her tongue. After all, the kids were there. And besides, it hardly seemed worth the trouble. *I should be thankful she bothered to show up at all,* Elizabeth thought.

Elizabeth stood up. "See you later, guys," she said, smiling at the children. Then she stuck her nose in the air and breezed by Jessica without a word.

Elizabeth walked quickly down the hall and headed for the back door, getting more and more furious by the minute. It was bad enough that Jessica had shown up almost three hours late, but now she was competing with Elizabeth for the children's affection as well. Elizabeth shook her head in disgust.

Once she was outside, Elizabeth took long, deep breaths to calm herself. What she needed was a long, quiet walk away from the kids and away from her sister. Elizabeth glanced warily at the sky. Despite the earlier sunshine, it looked like a storm was approaching. The air was cool and damp, and a wind seemed to be picking up. Big black clouds hung threateningly in the sky.

A cold wind whipped through the trees, and Elizabeth shivered. She was dressed for summer, in a long, wraparound Indian print cotton skirt and an ivory T-shirt. Elizabeth hesitated, wondering if she should run upstairs and grab a jacket. But she didn't want to go back inside and risk facing Jessica again. Then she shrugged. Dinner was in less than an hour, so she wouldn't have time for more than a short walk anyway.

Elizabeth ducked her head and walked rapidly toward the forest, her heart heavy. She didn't know when she'd been so unhappy. First Todd dumped her, and now Jessica was turning on her. Elizabeth sighed deeply. She felt all alone in the world.

A deep bolt of thunder rumbled in the distance, agreeing with Elizabeth's black mood. Elizabeth hurried into the woods, hoping the approaching storm would hold off for an hour. It was damp and calm in the dense forest, and the smell of wet pinecones filled the air. Elizabeth walked quickly along the winding dirt path, taking deep breaths of the cool, fresh air.

After many twisting turns the path led out of the forest, and she found herself at a new entrance to the topiary maze. Elizabeth peeked into the tunnel of trees, feeling an almost irresistible urge to go inside it. She was sure she could take it back to the other side, to the meadow leading to the Château d'Amour Inconnu. Elizabeth hesitated a moment, then pressed on. Now that she wasn't chasing Pierre, she'd be careful to remember which turns she had taken.

Elizabeth felt a twinge of excitement as she entered the thick labyrinth of trees. The hedges blanketed her against the wind, and it was strangely silent in the maze. Elizabeth imagined herself as a princess slipping away for a few stolen moments of solitude. *What would a princess be thinking about right now?* she wondered. "True love, of course," she murmured aloud, answering her own question.

Obviously I'm not a princess, Elizabeth thought with a scowl, taking a turn to the right.

As she followed the damp path her mind drifted to Todd. *What's he doing right now?* she asked herself. She pictured him at the beach, playing volleyball on the sand with the guys. Or maybe he was alone on the basketball court, practicing his layups. Or maybe he was out on a date with another girl. . . .

Elizabeth shook the thought away. *Think positively,* she commanded herself. For all she knew, Todd was sitting alone in the park, thinking about her.

Does he miss me? she wondered, tears coming to her eyes. *Is he sorry that we broke up?* A tear slipped down her cheek, and Elizabeth wiped it quickly away.

Drawing a shaky breath, Elizabeth blinked back her tears. She reached another fork in the path and turned to the right again. Then she hesitated. Was the château to the right or the left? She looked around in all directions, realizing that she was totally disoriented. She'd lost her way once again.

How could you be so stupid? she berated herself. As she tried to find her bearings a bolt of thunder rocked the sky, and raindrops began to fall.

"Oh, great!" she grumbled, hugging her arms around herself. Now she was wet *and* lost. And it was getting dark. Feeling nervous, Elizabeth ran quickly to the left. After all, she reassured herself, she didn't have to find the château exit. She just had to find a way out of the maze. Elizabeth ran faster and faster, getting more and more scared.

The rain fell harder, causing the path under her feet to turn to mud. Panicked, Elizabeth began running blindly, sloshing through the maze in her soggy sandals. After a few minutes her clothes were soaked and she found herself shivering uncontrollably.

I'll never find my way out of here, she thought anxiously. She heard a sharp crack of thunder, and a flash of lightning zipped through the sky. A cold wind whipped through the trees, shooting big drops of rain into her face. "This is a nightmare!" she whimpered to herself, wrapping her arms around her body again. She could catch pneumonia. Or get electrocuted. Now Elizabeth was truly terrified.

Another flash of lightning shot through the sky and lit up the area for a second. Through the hedges Elizabeth caught a quick glimpse of a small cottage. Her whole body trembled in relief. She charged directly through the hedges to the clearing, scratching her bare arms on the branches.

But Elizabeth was oblivious to the pain. Breathing hard, she flew across the wet grass and pounded on the door of the cottage. *Please, please, let someone be here,* she said to herself. Otherwise she was doomed.

"Are you still working, Jessica?" Princess Catherine asked, popping her head into the nursery on Tuesday evening.

Jessica looked up at the sound of the princess's voice. Jessica was kneeling on the floor, stacking up a pile of board games. "I was just cleaning," she explained. The nursery was almost all tidied up, and the children were bathed and tucked into their beds. Getting them to bed had been a harrowing ordeal in itself.

The princess gave her a kind smile. "Well, everything looks perfect," she said. "Why don't you relax and enjoy yourself for the evening?"

Jessica flashed her a grateful smile, and the princess shut the door behind her.

"Finally!" Jessica muttered after the princess left the room. She carried the stack of games across the room and placed them carefully on the shelf. She was exhausted after playing with the children all evening, and she was starving as well. The kids had been so boisterous at dinner that Jessica had barely been able to take a bite.

Jessica leaned her head against the wall and closed her eyes. All she wanted to do was crawl into her bed and fall into a deep sleep. For once her tiny attic room seemed appealing. But her stomach was growling insistently. Jessica forced her eyes open and dragged herself to the kitchen.

The head chef was busy at the stove. A couple of steak filets were sizzling in a pan, and the rich smells of a chocolate cake came from the oven. Obviously he was preparing a gourmet dinner for the royal couple and their guests.

Jessica wandered over to him. "Is there anything left to eat?" she asked him.

The cook looked annoyed at being interrupted and snapped at her in French.

Jessica bit her lip. "Um, *répétez, s'il vous plaît?*"

she said, asking him to repeat what he had said.

The chef pointed to a covered pot on the stove and grumbled, "Beef."

Jessica smiled and lifted the lid. *Ah!* she thought, recognizing the dish as beef bourguignon. She ladled out a heaping plateful. Then she grabbed a bottle of soda from the refrigerator and carried everything to the table.

Jessica took a hungry bite out of her meal. "Mmm," she murmured appreciatively. This was much better than the pasta the children had eaten earlier.

Just then Anna breezed into the kitchen, a blouse and sewing supplies in her hand. She said something to the cook in French, then she joined Jessica at the table. "The job—it goes well?" she asked Jessica.

Jessica rolled her eyes dramatically. "I'm learning," she admitted. She wiped her mouth with her napkin and took a sip of her soda.

Anna smiled and patted her hand. "The children are very spirited, but they're loving and kind. They will respond to you soon enough."

"I hope so," Jessica said. "They're sweet, but they're exhausting." She dipped her fork into her food and blew on it.

Anna laid the blouse on the table. Then she ripped off a piece of thread and knotted it adeptly. "Is it difficult being so far from home?" she asked.

Jessica shrugged. "No, it's OK," she said

thoughtfully. "I miss my friends and my family, but it's nice to get away for a change." She brought her fork to her lips and took a big bite.

"So you did not leave a handsome boyfriend behind?" Anna asked. Her round brown eyes twinkled mischievously.

Jessica swallowed and shook her head. "No. I was dating a guy named Cameron, but it didn't work out." Jessica had met Cameron Smith during her internship as an assistant to the head photographer at *Flair* magazine. They had gone out for a while, but eventually the relationship had fizzled out. Cameron had to travel all the time on business, and they rarely got to see each other.

"Oh, that is too bad," Anna said. She opened her sewing kit and picked out a small blue button. Then she sewed it on the shirt with nimble fingers.

"Well, I did meet a fascinating guy on the train," Jessica ventured.

Anna dropped the shirt on the table. "You don't waste any time, do you?"

Jessica shook her head with a laugh. Then she leaned in close to Anna. "What do you know about the son of the duke of Norveaux?" she asked.

Anna tipped her head, visibly confused. "There is no duke of Norveaux," she said.

Jessica frowned. "What do you mean?"

Anna shrugged. "Well, as far as I know, Norveaux doesn't exist."

"Maybe you've just never heard of it?" Jessica suggested.

But Anna shook her head firmly. "I'm afraid not. France isn't a very big country, and the regions have been established for a long time." Then she laughed. "Poor Jessica. You've obviously run into a dashing French rogue with a silver tongue."

Jessica's stomach dropped to her feet. *Is it possible that Jacques lied to me?* she wondered. She thought of his flirtatious lines, his smooth jokes, his seductive accent. . . . *It's more than possible,* she realized finally.

"Don't be sad," Anna told her. "In France everything is forgiven if it is for love. Maybe this young fellow wanted badly to impress you."

"For love," Jessica muttered, lowering her eyes.

Jessica pushed her food around on her plate with her fork, angry with herself for being so stupid. She didn't think Jacques had lied to her for love. He was probably just looking for a fun time on the train. After all, the jewel he gave her was just a cheap piece of junk. Suddenly she felt sick to her stomach.

"I'm too tired to eat anymore," Jessica said, quickly pushing her chair back and standing up. "If you'll excuse me."

Anna followed her with worried eyes. "Good night, Jessica," she said softly.

Jessica climbed the long, winding steps to her tiny attic room and pushed open the door. Without bothering to turn on the light, she threw herself across her bed. She felt totally dejected. Nothing was working out right.

I'm treated like a servant around here, Jessica thought. *Elizabeth hates me. I burned an important letter. I'm a terrible baby-sitter. And Jacques turns out to be a jerk!*

Jessica sat up and folded her arms, tears stinging in her eyes. "Life is so unfair!"

Chapter 10

Prince Laurent opened the door of his cottage, and an electric current coursed through his body. Standing before him was the blond girl from his dream. Startled, he stood rooted to the spot, his heart pounding.

"Can I please come in?" she demanded in English, trembling.

Suddenly Laurent realized that the girl was soaked to the skin and shivering violently. Obviously she was very real—and in distress.

"Oh, excuse me!" Laurent exclaimed, responding in English as well. He held open the door and ushered her inside, kicking himself for thinking she was a mirage. *She must be one of the au pairs,* he realized suddenly. *Otherwise she wouldn't be speaking English.*

"Please, follow me," he said, leading her to a

small, rustic den. A thick red throw rug covered the wooden floor, and a bright fire crackled in the hearth.

"Why don't you warm up by the fire?" he suggested. She smiled at him gratefully and sank down on the rug in front of the fire. Laurent glanced at her in wonder, then he rushed off to find some towels.

When he returned, the sight of her startled him all over again. Framed by the fire's glow, she was kneeling with her hands outstretched. Her heart-shaped face was flushed pink and her lips curled in a soft smile. Something in Laurent's heart stirred, as if warmed by the same fire.

She turned to him at that moment, and Laurent felt his heart melt completely.

"Um, are those for me?" she asked with a small grin.

"Oh, right! Yes!" he said, hurrying toward her and handing her a stack of fluffy blue towels. He didn't know what had come over him. Usually he was calm and in control, and now he was falling to pieces.

"Thank you," she said, accepting them gratefully. She wiped off her arms and rubbed a towel briskly through her wet hair. Laurent sat down in an armchair by the corner of the rug, trying not to stare at her.

The girl wrapped the towel turban style around her head, and Laurent glanced at her admiringly. Now she looked even more like a princess than ever. Her eyes glittered like sapphires, and her wide cheekbones stood out in her luminescent face. Laurent's stomach fluttered strangely.

"I'm Elizabeth Wakefield," she said with a smile. "I'm working at the château as an au pair for the summer."

Laurent nodded and smiled back. "That is what I guessed," he said. "Most French girls don't speak perfect English." He pushed a lock of dark hair off his forehead. "I'm Laurent, the oldest de Sainte-Marie."

"I know," the girl admitted, a sheepish grin on her face. "I saw you yesterday when you were practicing with your sword." She blushed suddenly and looked down. "Pierre is a bit devilish at times," she explained. "He ran into the maze, and I had to go in after him. I finally found him by the hedges in front of the cottage."

So I didn't imagine her after all, Prince Laurent realized, somewhat relieved. *She really did disappear into the maze.*

Elizabeth shivered, and Laurent jumped up quickly. "You're still cold," he said. He grabbed a thick red blanket from the sofa and knelt down next to her. "Here," he said, handing her the blanket. "Try to warm up a bit."

Elizabeth wrapped the blanket tightly around her shoulders and smiled at him gratefully.

Laurent smiled back and stood up. "Uh, I'll go make you a pot of tea," he said, backing out of the room awkwardly.

Laurent rushed to the kitchen and quickly put on a kettle of water. He was completely shaken up.

Even if he hadn't imagined Elizabeth in the maze, he *had* dreamed about her. He was sure of it. She had the same golden blond hair and the same ocean blue eyes as the mysterious girl in his dream. It was uncanny.

A few minutes later Laurent returned to the den with a steaming pot of tea and two china cups. He quickly poured Elizabeth a cup and sat down opposite her.

Elizabeth took a sip of hot tea and set down the cup. Her hair hung loose around her shoulders now, and her face was glowing. "What a relief!" she exclaimed. "I feel a hundred times better." She shook her head. "I was worried I would never get out of the maze."

"It's a lot more complicated than it looks," Laurent said. "I used to play in it for hours and hours as a little boy."

Elizabeth grinned. "Just like Pierre!" she said.

Laurent nodded. "But *my* nannies never found me!" he said with a wink.

After Elizabeth had finished her cup of tea, she stood up. "I should be getting back to the château," she said. "I'm already late for dinner."

At that moment a bolt of thunder crashed through the sky, followed by a streak of lightning. Elizabeth bit her lip, going to the window and pulling back the curtain. Laurent got up and joined her. It was dark outside, and a steady stream of rain was pouring down. "I hope there's an easier route than the maze," Elizabeth said.

Laurent shook his head. "There's a dirt road that loops around the estate, but it's probably flooded. And the maze is out of the question. Even *I* couldn't find my way through it in this weather."

Elizabeth looked at him, worry in her clear blue-green eyes. "What am I going to do?" she asked softly.

"You'll have to stay here with me tonight," Laurent decided.

And let me take care of you, Laurent added to himself. He only wished the rain would never stop.

Hours later Elizabeth was curled up in a heavy blanket on the couch, sipping hot cider. She and Laurent were in a small sitting room with big bay windows and wooden ceiling beams. A warm fire burned in the hearth, casting an orange glow about the cozy room.

Prince Laurent was telling her about some of the childhood pranks he had pulled on his baby-sitters. He spoke almost perfect English, with just the slightest French accent. With his smooth, chiseled features and jet-black hair, he looked every bit the refined noble. But when he talked, everything about him changed. His deep blue eyes crinkled and his face lit up, giving him a warm, mischievous air. Elizabeth found herself completely entranced by him.

"One summer I had a young British girl as an au pair," he said. "She was very polite and very timid. I made up a legend about a headless horse-man, and then one night I rode in front of her window on my horse. I was wearing a sheet and carrying a dummy's head in my hand. I've never heard anybody scream so loud." He grinned sheepishly. "She left the next day."

"That's despicable," Elizabeth said, laughing. "Compared to you, Pierre, Claudine, and Manon are perfect angels!" Elizabeth took a sip of cider, shaking her head. "In fact, I'm surprised you're even related."

A shadow crossed Laurent's face suddenly, and his expression turned serious. "Well, they're only my half siblings," he said.

Elizabeth looked at him quizzically.

"My mother died when I was ten," Laurent said quietly. "She drowned in a boat accident on the Mediterranean Sea."

Elizabeth gasped. "How horrible!" she exclaimed sympathetically.

Laurent nodded. "I know," he said. He picked up his mug of cider and took a sip, a pensive look on his face. "But you know, somehow it was comforting to me that she died at sea." Laurent was quiet for a moment. Then he stood up and walked to the window, pulling back the curtain and gazing out the window. "My mother was a creature of the water. She grew up on the coast of France and spend her childhood sailing and waterskiing." Laurent walked across the room, deep in thought.

"It was like she returned to her natural habitat." Then he looked embarrassed and scuffed his foot along the floor. "I've never told anybody that before," he said.

"Was she your father's first love?" Elizabeth asked softly.

Laurent frowned. "I think so, or at least I *thought* so," he corrected himself. He shook his head and walked to the fire, picking up an iron poker. "It's the strangest thing. I just found out that my father and Catherine were friends before he married my mother." Laurent shrugged and stoked the fire. "Who knows? Maybe they were in love way back then."

Elizabeth was quiet, caught up in Laurent's tale. But suddenly Laurent turned around and faced her, a small smile on his lips. "And do you know what's even stranger?"

Elizabeth shook her head. "What?"

"When my father was my age, he refused the throne and tried to establish a more equitable political system. He was a sort of revolutionary."

Elizabeth's mouth dropped open. "Prince Nicolas? A revolutionary?"

"I didn't believe it myself," Laurent said with a laugh.

Elizabeth was pensive. "You know, that's funny. My mother was exactly the same in the seventies. She was a bit of a radical herself. She organized peace marches and political rallies—"

"And she had long hair and wore colored beads around her neck," Laurent finished for her.

Elizabeth laughed along with him. "Exactly!" she said.

Laurent's expression softened, and he caught her eyes in his. Elizabeth felt suddenly light-headed, as if she were flying.

Laurent sat down across from her on the couch. "You know, Elizabeth, I feel like I've known you forever," he said quietly.

Elizabeth nodded. "I feel the same way," she whispered.

Suddenly a bird tweeted and a faint golden light shone through the white lace curtains. Laurent went to the window and pulled them open. The sun was just appearing over the horizon. Elizabeth stared at it in disbelief. They'd been up all night, talking and laughing.

"Good morning," Laurent said, facing her with a smile. "It looks like it's going to be a beautiful day."

"It does," Elizabeth agreed. The sky was bright and clear, and there wasn't a cloud in sight.

"I know you're anxious to get back to my angelic siblings," Laurent joked, "but what about breakfast first? I make a very terrific cheese omelette."

Elizabeth raised her eyebrows. "I've been rescued by a prince who can cook?" she declared. "I am one lucky damsel in distress."

"Does that mean you accept my offer?" Laurent asked.

Elizabeth nodded with a laugh.

"Right this way, my damsel in distress," Laurent said, leading her down the hall.

The kitchen was small and cozy, just like the rest of the wooden cottage. The floor was covered in faded red tiles, and the walls were painted a pale green. Potted plants lined the windowsill.

"Let me help you," Elizabeth said.

"Absolutely not," Laurent refused with a shake of his head. "Today is your day off." He pointed to a chair sternly.

Elizabeth smiled and sat down at the round wooden table in the corner. She rested her chin on her hand and watched him prepare breakfast. Laurent tied a white apron around his waist and plopped a big white chef's cap on his head. Then he gave Elizabeth a deep bow. "Chef Laurent, at your service!"

Elizabeth couldn't help chuckling. Grabbing a handful of eggs from the refrigerator, Laurent proceeded to juggle them in the air. He flipped an egg behind his back and caught it in one hand. "That's to impress the visiting au pair," he said with a wink. Then he cracked the eggs against a bowl and mixed them with a fork.

A few minutes later a big Spanish omelette was sizzling in a frying pan. "Now we are going to fleep zee omelette," Laurent said, exaggerating his own accent. "Just like they do in the movies." With that he whisked the pan off the stove and flipped the omelette into the air, catching it smoothly on a big plate. He set the plate in front of Elizabeth with a flourish. "At your service, my princess." He bowed low again.

Elizabeth giggled as he joined her at the table. *Laurent keeps showing me new sides of himself,* she thought. He was obviously quite complex. He was serious, deep, funny, and silly all at the same time. *He's a lot like me,* Elizabeth realized with a start.

Laurent cut the omelette in half and served her. *"Bon appétit!"* he said.

"Bon appétit!" Elizabeth responded, cutting into the omelette and taking a bite.

Elizabeth sat back and took a sip of fresh-roasted coffee, feeling at peace for the first time since she'd arrived on the island. She'd never met a boy she felt so comfortable with. *Except Todd,* she silently reminded herself. But she pushed the thought out of her mind. *He hasn't tried to get in touch with me,* she thought. *Todd is history.*

Besides, she and Laurent were just friends. Obviously that was why she felt so comfortable with him. But she looked into his dark blue eyes, and her heart fluttered.

We are *just friends,* she told herself. *Aren't we?*

Where are you, Liz? Jessica worried on Wednesday morning, her heart in her throat. *Where are you?* She had been repeating the words all morning.

She was trying to supervise the kids at break-fast, but her mind was a blur of panic. She didn't have any idea where Elizabeth had gone. And she had no idea how long she'd been missing. Jessica had only noticed her disappearance this morning.

When she told the prince and princess de Sainte-Marie about her sister's absence, they assured her that Elizabeth was OK. "She probably took shelter from the storm in one of the cottages or huts on the estate," the princess had said. They promised to send some workers to look for her if she didn't return by midmorning.

But that could be too late, Jessica thought worriedly. *Elizabeth could be lying in a ditch, hurt and bleeding, right now.* Her tongue went dry at the thought.

"Jessica, can I have another croissant?" Claudine asked.

Jessica nodded and handed her the bread basket absently. She pushed back her chair and went to the window, willing her sister to appear. But all that greeted her eyes were long, clear stretches of meadow. Elizabeth was nowhere to be seen.

Elizabeth, please be OK, Jessica pleaded silently to the empty fields. She only hoped that Elizabeth hadn't gotten lost in the storm the night before. *Maybe she fell down in the forest and hurt herself,* Jessica thought. *Or maybe she was attacked by a wild animal.* Then a horrible thought struck her. What if Elizabeth had gone into the ocean by herself?

Jessica bit her lip, tears coming to her eyes. If anything had happened to her sister, it would be all her fault. After all, Jessica was the one who had upset her yesterday. If Elizabeth had taken off in the storm, it was because of Jessica.

Finally Jessica decided she couldn't stand it any longer. She had to go out and look for her sister. She would just have to bring the children with her.

"C'mon, kids," Jessica said, clapping sharply. "Let's get the table cleaned up. Pronto!"

"Pronto!" Pierre said with a giggle, imitating the new word.

After the table was cleared, Jessica mopped up the children's hands and faces and herded them outdoors. The day was calm and clear, and everything was fresh and glistening from the rain. But the ground was still damp, and all three kids promptly ran for the muddy puddles. Pierre splashed about wildly, kicking dirty water at Claudine. Claudine shouted in pleasure, jumping up and down in a puddle.

"Chil-dren!" Jessica called, running after them. Just as she reached the puddle, the Countess di Rimini and Antonia walked by. The countess lifted her waxed-thin eyebrows as she took in the sight of the children playing in the mud. Then she pursed her lips, muttering something in French to Antonia.

Jessica had no idea what she had said, but she flashed her a wry smile. "The same to you," she replied.

The countess gasped and rushed off in a huff with her daughter. Jessica made a face behind their backs.

Claudine and Pierre snickered, making nasty faces at the di Riminis as well. The children tried to outdo each other, sticking their tongues out and putting their thumbs in their ears.

Jessica rolled her eyes. "You kids are too much."

"Mademoiselle Elizabeth!" Manon cried suddenly, pointing across the yard.

Jessica whirled around and saw her twin sauntering toward them. Elizabeth looked relaxed and happy, whistling as she headed across the meadow. Jessica's whole body trembled with relief, and she flew across the lawn to meet her.

"What in the world happened?" Jessica demanded when she reached her. "I was worried sick about you!"

"I got lost in the maze, trying to find my way back to the castle, and then the storm started," Elizabeth explained. "Fortunately I stumbled on Prince Laurent's cottage, and he let me stay there for the night."

Jessica's eyes widened, her curiosity piqued. "The prince? What's he like?"

Elizabeth shrugged. "He's nice," she replied evasively.

Jessica raised an eyebrow, wondering if there was more to the story than Elizabeth was letting on. But she'd have to press her for details later. "Well, all that matters is that you're all right,"

Jessica said. She hugged her sister close, tears coming to her eyes. "I was so scared, Liz," she said in a throaty voice. "You're the only twin I've got." Jessica pulled back, sniffing. "Promise me you won't run off again without letting me know first?"

Elizabeth nodded, her eyes glistening with tears as well. "I promise." Then she smiled. "Hey, does this mean we're talking to each other again?"

Jessica nodded. She had been so worried that she had completely forgotten about their fight. And now she realized how stupid it was. She also recognized how selfish she had been. Elizabeth was going through a really hard time. The least Jessica could do was support her. "Let's stop being mad at each other, Liz," Jessica said. "Our fight was totally idiotic."

"I couldn't agree more," Elizabeth replied.

Jessica looked down at the ground. "Elizabeth, I'm sorry. I guess I *was* sort of shirking my duties."

"Well, now I've made up for it, right?" Elizabeth said.

Jessica grinned. "That's right! You missed breakfast duty!"

Elizabeth leaned back and looked into Jessica's eyes. "Friends?" she asked.

"Friends," Jessica murmured.

Jessica felt like a weight had been lifted from her. Linking arms with her sister, she walked with her toward the garden, where the children were playing.

But on their way back to the castle Jessica was

struck with a horrible thought—Elizabeth's letter! *What was I thinking?* Jessica berated herself. *Now the letter is gone, and there's no way to get it back.*

Now that she and Elizabeth had made up, Jessica felt terribly guilty. Elizabeth was miserable about Todd. Nothing would make her happier than to receive a letter from him.

Jessica bit her lip and turned to her sister. She had to tell her about the letter from Todd. At least Elizabeth would know that Todd was thinking about her. Elizabeth smiled warmly at Jessica and slung an arm around her shoulders.

Jessica turned away. She just couldn't bring herself to confess. If Elizabeth knew what she had done, she might never forgive her.

He'll write again, Jessica assured herself.

Chapter 11

Elizabeth hummed to herself as she wandered through the wild English garden behind the château on Friday evening. It was a warm, balmy evening, and the sun was setting over the horizon, casting a pink glow over the meadows. Red and yellow tulips lined the white stone path, and beds of miniature pink roses were clustered on either side.

The prince and princess were hosting a formal dinner party that evening at the château, and the entire household was involved in a flurry of preparations. Elizabeth was glad to escape from the chaos during her break from the children. Although the twins had made up, they had decided to keep up their system of trading off shifts. Elizabeth was scheduled to take over shortly, and she'd have the kids until bedtime.

Swinging her arms, Elizabeth strolled along the

stone path. She came upon a narrow, gurgling brook surrounded by fields of red and blue wildflowers. She stopped in awe, marveling at the natural beauty of the landscape. It seemed as if every day she discovered something new on the property. Bending down, Elizabeth picked a tiny bunch of red wildflowers.

Elizabeth whistled as she continued along the path, her spirits high. She had been at the château for almost a week now, and she was beginning to get accustomed to the lifestyle. In fact, ever since she had met Laurent, she felt at peace with the world. She and Jessica were getting along, and even the kids were behaving better. The summer was turning out to be more fun than she had expected.

Elizabeth heard a man's voice humming softly, and her heart leapt. She hadn't seen Laurent since Tuesday night, but she knew he'd be coming to the château for the royal dinner.

She hesitated for a moment. Then she headed in the direction of the sound, her heart beating faster in her chest.

She turned the corner and peeked around it. Henri, the gardener, was crouched among the flowering bushes, shearing the plants and pulling weeds. He was humming a soft tune as he worked. Elizabeth shook her head, laughing at herself for her false hopes.

"*Bonsoir,* mademoiselle," Henri said, wishing her a good evening.

"*Bonsoir*, Henri," Elizabeth responded politely.

Then he pointed to her bouquet of flowers, a glint in his light brown eyes. "You have picked those for me?" he asked in broken English.

Elizabeth nodded and handed them to him. "I picked them just for you," she said.

Henri put a hand to his heart. "Mademoiselle, I am touched," he said.

Elizabeth laughed as she walked away, but she couldn't help feeling disappointed. Then she shook her head hard. *I'm not hoping to run into Prince Laurent,* she told herself. *Not at all.* Her decision to take a walk had *nothing* to do with the fact that Laurent was expected at the château that evening.

Although she'd had a wonderful time with him the other night, she didn't think anything would come of it. Why would Laurent want to get involved with an American girl who lived all the way across the sea? And why should she think he was interested in her anyway? Just because he took care of her the other night didn't mean anything. After all, it was the gentlemanly thing to do. And Laurent was certainly a gentleman.

It's a good thing I'm not interested in him, Elizabeth thought firmly. The path forked and she turned to the right, coming upon a fallen tree. Elizabeth grabbed onto a branch and climbed over the tree trunk. *Besides,* she thought, *it's too soon to go out with somebody else.* She needed time to heal after her breakup with Todd.

Elizabeth followed the path out of the garden, recalling their last moments together at Lila's party. She thought of Todd's discomfort, of his cold words, of the pain in her heart. . . . . But somehow the memory didn't hurt very much now, Elizabeth realized with surprise. It seemed as if it had all happened ages ago, in another lifetime. Sweet Valley felt very far away.

Elizabeth ducked under a low tree branch and walked out into the meadow. Then she froze in her tracks. Prince Laurent was headed straight toward her, trotting on a beautiful white stallion. Next to him was a black mare, which he was leading by the reins. Laurent looked more handsome than ever on the majestic animal.

Elizabeth gazed at him, breathless. "A prince on a white horse," she whispered to herself. For a moment she felt as if she'd slipped into a romantic fairy tale.

Get real! she ordered herself with a swift mental kick. She clenched her hands together behind her back and ordered herself to stop acting like a fool.

Laurent pulled at the reins and brought the horses to a stop by her side.

"*Bonsoir,* Laurent," Elizabeth said, forcing her voice to sound casual.

Laurent looked into her eyes. "You're not surprised to see me," he remarked.

Elizabeth tipped her head, bemused. "I figured you'd be coming to the château for your parents' party."

He stared at her blankly for a moment, then groaned. "The party!" he said, hitting himself on the side of the head. "I'd forgotten all about it!"

"Well, aren't you glad that I reminded you, then?" Elizabeth asked.

Laurent shook his head with a smile. "Actually it doesn't matter, because I've already made other plans—and they're much too important to cancel for a formal dinner party."

Elizabeth eyed him suspiciously. "What sort of plans?" she asked.

"Would you like to take a ride with me and find out?" he challenged.

Elizabeth hesitated. It was her turn to take the kids, and her shift would be starting shortly. Jessica would kill her if she didn't show up for dinner. On the other hand, Elizabeth thought, she loved horseback riding. And a handsome prince on a white horse was inviting her to go for a ride.

Elizabeth grinned to herself. Obviously no decision was necessary. Jessica could definitely handle the kids for a few more hours. Nothing was going to keep her from hanging out with Laurent.

"I think I'd like that very much," she said quickly. She put a foot into the saddle and climbed onto the black mare.

"Follow me!" Laurent said, turning his horse around and kicking his flanks lightly. The horse burst into a gallop and sped across the fields. "Whoa, Pardaillan!" Laurent exclaimed, bringing the horse to a stop and twisting around in his saddle.

Her heart beating in excitement, Elizabeth tapped lightly on her horse's sides. The black mare broke into a steady trot and Elizabeth tightened her grip on the reins, getting accustomed to the horse's movement.

"You ready to go?" he asked when she joined him.

Elizabeth smiled, her cheeks flushed. "Ready," she said.

And they were off.

"Pierre, stop playing with your food!" Jessica ordered as Pierre juggled a warm roll at the kitchen table on Friday evening. The roll flew out of his little hands and bounced across the table, falling onto the floor. "You see?" she said. "Now you can't eat it."

Pierre shrugged. "I'm not hungry anyway," he said.

"Well, then, why don't you play with your new toy set?" Jessica suggested, leaning over to retrieve the roll. The prince and princess had given Pierre a set of miniature plastic soldiers, and he had been playing with them all day.

Elizabeth, where are *you?* Jessica muttered to herself as she set the roll on the table. Elizabeth hadn't shown up for her shift yet, so Jessica was taking her sister's dinner duty. The children were having spaghetti and meatballs, but they were more interested in playing with their food than eating it. They were in a particularly rambunctious mood this evening, obviously wound up by the excitement in the air.

Pierre set two little toy soldiers on the table. "Bam, bam, bam!" he yelled out, marching one of them across the table.

Claudine scooped up the other soldier and positioned it behind Pierre's bowl. "Pow!" she returned.

"This is war!" Pierre yelled, picking up his soldier and making it leap into his bowl of spaghetti. Claudine quickly followed suit, stationing her soldier on a meatball. The children burst out into hysterical laughter as their soldiers fought in the field of pasta.

Jessica clapped sharply. "OK, that's enough!" she said.

"But you said I could play—" Pierre whined, crossing his arms over his chest.

"Well, I didn't mean in your food," Jessica interrupted. She grabbed the soldiers and wiped them off with her napkin. "You can play when you've finished eating."

Pierre stuck out his lower lip and stared down at his food. Pouting, he wound up a forkful of spaghetti and brought it to his mouth. Then he picked up a long strand with his fingers and pasted it above his lip, curling it into a mustache.

Claudine burst out laughing.

"Pi-erre!" Jessica groaned.

Pierre looked at her innocently, sucking the pasta into his mouth. "You don't like my mustache?" he asked.

Jessica shook her head, hiding a grin. "Well, you're a little bit young," she said.

"I almost have six years!" Pierre shouted out.

"I *am* almost six years old," Jessica corrected him.

Manon banged her hands on her tray. Then she picked up one of the toy soldiers and brought it to her mouth.

"Manon! That's for playing, not eating," Jessica said, gently disengaging the soldier from her mouth.

Jessica sighed and glanced at the antique clock on the kitchen wall. Elizabeth was over an hour late, and Jessica was beginning to get worried.

She had tried to find out if anyone had seen her sister, but everybody was preoccupied with the preparations for the royal dinner party. The entire kitchen staff was in a frenzy, as if they were getting ready to launch a space rocket instead of a dinner party. The head chef was in the kitchen barking out orders to the other cooks, and caterers were bustling around with platters of food.

Even Anna didn't have a moment for her. She was whirling around the house like a tornado, frantically taking care of last-minute details. Every time she passed through the kitchen, she had something else in her hand. On her last trip she had swept through the room carrying a long, unrolled scroll with the guest list on it. Jessica had tried to grab her, but Anna hadn't even stopped to look at her. "I'll be with you in a minute, Jessica!" she had promised on her way out the door. That was half an hour ago.

Jessica sighed and slumped down in her seat, feeling completely helpless. Nobody would talk to her, and she couldn't go out to look for Elizabeth herself because of the children. Jessica puffed her cheeks out in frustration.

The back door slammed shut suddenly, and Jessica sat up quickly. She listened for the sound of her sister's voice, but she couldn't make anything out over the buzz of the kitchen staff.

Jessica pushed back her chair and jumped up, grabbing the soldiers in her hand. "You guys, make sure Manon doesn't put anything else in her mouth, OK?" she said.

The kids nodded, and Jessica hurried across the room. She really hoped it was her twin because she didn't think she could handle one more minute of the children.

The entire household staff was in a frenzy in the kitchen. The head chef was preparing oysters at the stove, and Fernand was at the counter, rolling dough on a cutting board. Caterers were hurrying to and fro, carrying trays of exotic-looking hors d'oeuvres. The sweet smell of an apple tart wafted from the oven. Jessica inched her way through the kitchen, trying not to disturb the staff.

Suddenly she collided with a big platter of hors d'oeuvres lifted in the air.

"*Excusez-moi,*" Jessica exclaimed, jumping back.

The caterer lowered her arm and looked at Jessica with pursed lips. "Tut-tut-tut," she clicked.

The head chef muttered something under his breath in French, and the woman agreed.

"Sorry," Jessica said, backing up a few feet.

The woman lifted the tray high above her head and swept away.

Just then Henri walked into the room, wearing a light blue jacket. He was carrying a pair of garden shears and a small bouquet of red wildflowers.

Jessica's face fell when she saw him. Obviously he had just come in from outside.

"Good evening, Mademoiselle Jessica," he said, bowing his head politely. "You look sad. Perhaps you were expecting someone else?"

"Actually, I was," Jessica replied. "I was hoping you were my sister. I'm afraid she might have gotten lost again."

Henri smiled broadly. "If she is lost, then she is not lost alone."

"Huh?" Jessica asked.

"I saw Elizabeth ride off with Prince Laurent on a horse," he informed her.

Jessica's jaw dropped. "Are you sure?" she asked.

"It is not possible," Fernand put in from the stove in English, where he was stirring a rich-smelling cream sauce. "Prince Laurent is expected for dinner, and the first course will be served in less than an hour." He dipped a wooden spoon into his sauce and sniffed at it. "Prince Laurent will certainly not miss such an affair."

Henri shrugged. "I do not know about that. He

had a basket with him." He reached up into a cabinet for a vase. "It seems he has already taken care of their dinner."

"Mais, ce n'est pas possible!" the head chef burst out, waving his arms around in an agitated manner. Then he spoke in rapid-fire French to Fernand.

Fernand shook his head in disapproval and stirred his sauce harder. Henri shrugged and filled the vase with water.

How could she do this to me? Jessica fumed silently.

When she returned to the table, she found the kids were building a model village across the table with their food. They had fashioned little round huts out of mounds of spaghetti, with chimneys made out of meatballs. Now they were constructing a forest out of broccoli stalks and carrots.

Elizabeth, I'm going to strangle you, Jessica vowed.

Pierre looked up, beaming proudly. "Do you like it?"

"Love it," Jessica grumbled. "Now let's clean this mess up or there won't be any dessert for you guys."

Giggling, the children scooped up the clumps of food with their hands.

Jessica started to protest, but then she stopped herself. At least the children were cleaning up. She just hoped they would raze their city before the royal couple arrived. She headed for the pantry to find something for dessert.

A number of caterers were in the pantry, preparing trays and speaking a mile a minute in French. Jessica pushed through the door and glanced at the shelves.

"Out, out!" one of the caterers yelled in English, shooing her away as if she were a fly.

"You again!" said the woman whom she had collided with earlier.

"But I promised the kids dessert," Jessica protested.

The woman grabbed a silver tray and shoved it at Jessica. The tray was filled with chocolate- and cheese-filled croissants that were left over from breakfast. "Stay out, mademoiselle," she ordered tersely.

Jessica scowled as she carried the croissants back to the children's table. It was bad enough that she wasn't invited to the party, but she was being completely abused by the staff as well. Plus she was stuck having to cover the evening shift with the royal monsters because her sister had ridden off with a prince.

"Here's dessert," Jessica announced, setting the tray on the table with a loud thud. The kids dove for the croissants, and Jessica barely batted an eye. Sighing, she sank down into her seat.

"Will Mademoiselle Elizabeth read the elephant book to us again tonight?" Pierre asked, stuffing a flaky chocolate-filled croissant in his mouth.

Jessica flashed him a brittle smile. "Who knows what she'll do?" she replied tightly. "Elizabeth is full of surprises."

"Surprises?" Claudine echoed cheerfully. "We love surprises."

Manon bounced in her seat, her face smeared with chocolate. "Surprises, surprises," she chanted happily.

I will strangle Elizabeth, Jessica thought hotly.

"This is wonderful, Laurent," Elizabeth declared as she ripped off another chunk of sourdough bread.

They were sitting on a blanket on the beach, sharing a picnic dinner. Laurent had prepared a gourmet meal with a selection of cold cuts, French cheeses, duck pâté, and fresh bread. He had also brought a jug of apple cider and two wineglasses.

"Even better than my omelette specialty?" Laurent asked with a grin.

Elizabeth nodded. "Well, it's a close second," she said. Then she gestured toward the ocean. "Actually, I was talking about the view." She spread some pâté on the bread and took a bite.

Stars were twinkling in the midnight sky, and the full moon was shining brightly above the eastern horizon. A short distance away the waves of the Mediterranean splashed rhythmically against the rocky shore.

"I thought you would be the sort of girl who would enjoy dining under the stars," Laurent said. He picked up her glass and refilled it.

Elizabeth smiled. "You thought right." She

gazed at the sea and sighed in contentment. "This is all so beautiful."

"Does it remind you of your home?" he asked.

Elizabeth thought for a moment, then shrugged. "In some ways it does," she admitted. "We come from southern California and live close to the beach. I'm used to warm summer nights and the smell of the sea in the air." She paused, deep in thought. "But you know, there's something different about the Mediterranean. It's more savage, somehow."

Laurent looked at her with interest. "Savage? What do you mean?"

"Well, there seems to be more of a contrast here," Elizabeth explained. "In California we have sand dunes and beaches on the ocean." She gestured out to sea. "But here there are huge white cliffs jutting into the water and giant mountain ranges in the distance." Elizabeth scooped up a handful of white pebbles and let them sift through her fingers. "And the beaches are covered with tiny stones." Elizabeth took a sip of her cider. "The island is more—" She paused as she searched for the right word. "Passionate," she said finally.

"Ah! Passion! Of course!" Laurent said with a grin. "That is because the island is French."

Elizabeth rolled her eyes. "And the moon? Is that French too?"

"Yes, of course," Laurent said. "Here in France we have our own moon." He looked at her with a matter-of-fact expression on his face.

Elizabeth shook her head, laughing.

"But it is true!" Laurent claimed, waving his arms around dramatically. "In France everything is unique—the cheese, the wine, the men, the moon!"

"Laurent, stop it!" Elizabeth said, laughing in earnest. He joined in with her, and soon they were laughing uproariously. After a few minutes she sat back, wiping tears out of her eyes. She realized she hadn't felt this relaxed in ages.

"I have never known anyone like you before," Laurent said quietly. He reached for her hand. For a moment they were silent, listening together to the lulling rhythm of the waves beating against the shore.

Then he gazed into her eyes and spoke in a whisper. "Elizabeth, there are things you don't know about me—things you *should* know."

But Elizabeth shook her head. She didn't want to spoil the mood. She curled her fingers around his and looked into his eyes. "I know everything I need to know—at least for this moment," she told him.

Laurent smiled and brushed her hair back from her face, his eyes intent and serious.

With a start she realized why he looked familiar when she first saw him. *The dream on the airplane,* she thought. She closed her eyes, remembering the details—how she'd been lost in a field of wildflowers until a handsome guy on a white horse had rescued her, a guy with jet-black hair and deep blue eyes. . . .

Laurent was the guy in my dream! Elizabeth

marveled. A thrilling sensation tingled up and down her spine. *Is Prince Laurent my destiny?* she wondered.

Late that evening Jessica dragged her body up the long, winding staircase to her room. She was exhausted after an entire day with the kids, and her legs felt like they weighed two tons each. Sounds of the party wafted up the steps from the salon. Classical music was playing, and guests were laughing quietly.

Jessica scowled fiercely. Not only was she tired, but she was furious. Everybody was having fun but her. She couldn't believe Elizabeth had skipped out on her duties for the entire evening. She deeply resented having had to cover her sister's shift. She had been hoping to go for a late night swim while the prince and princess entertained their guests.

Jessica grabbed onto the wooden banister and pulled herself around another turn. Breathing deeply, she plodded up the stone steps. "I'll never forgive her for this," she muttered through clenched teeth.

Of course, a nagging voice told her, *I often dump my work on Elizabeth.* In fact, she had shown up three hours late for her shift on Tuesday afternoon.

Then Jessica shrugged. *Elizabeth is* supposed *to be the responsible twin,* she reasoned. And Jessica hoped she would start acting like her old reliable self soon. The summer would be unbearable if her sister didn't shape up quickly.

Jessica reached her room and pushed open the door. It was pitch-dark inside and smelled damp and musty. Jessica felt along the dusty wall for the light switch, shivering unexpectedly. "This place gives me the creeps," she grumbled.

Suddenly a large hand gripped hers on the wall. Jessica gasped and let forth a scream. But then another hand covered her mouth, blanketing the sound.

Jessica felt as if her heart had stopped. Then it began to pound fiercely, sounding a drumroll in her chest. She reached for the door, trying to pull free, but a solid arm locked itself around her and pulled her farther into the room.

Don't panic, Jessica said to herself, her stomach coiling in fear. *Don't panic*. She forced herself to stand perfectly still. Then she gathered all her forces together and struggled wildly with her captor. But the arms were like a vise around her, and they kept tightening. Soon she couldn't move at all.

Jessica gasped for air, feeling as if she were suffocating. Her eyes wide with terror, she opened her mouth and screamed. But like in a nightmare, no sound came out.

I'm going to die, she thought.

Chapter 12

"There's a special place I want to show you," Laurent told Elizabeth as they were riding through the forest back to the château. The path narrowed, and Laurent guided his horse between the thick trees.

"This way, Cendrillon," Elizabeth directed, pulling lightly at the reins and directing her horse along the path.

Elizabeth sat back comfortably in the saddle, enjoying the steady movement of the mare's trot. It was peaceful and serene in the forest. The night air was cool and crisp, and fresh pine needles scented the air. She didn't know when she'd ever felt happier.

Elizabeth felt a twinge of guilt as she noticed the full moon above them. It was very late already. She had been gone for hours. Jessica was going to kill her. Elizabeth knew she really should be getting back soon.

Then Elizabeth shrugged. *You only live once,* she thought. Jessica was always telling her to loosen up, and now she was going to do it. For once she was going to choose the dream over reality. *Besides,* Elizabeth thought, *there's really no reason to go back now anyway.* The kids would already be in bed.

A small pond glimmered in the moonlight through the trees, and Laurent headed toward it. Elizabeth rode up next to him, pulling Cendrillon to a stop.

She caught her breath at the loveliness of the golden pond. Water lilies covered the surface, and huge weeping willows dipped into the edges. The moon beamed down on the water, making the surface glisten like a gold coin.

Laurent dismounted his horse and turned to her, his arms outstretched. Elizabeth put a foot in the stirrup and swung her leg over the horse's body. Taking her lightly by the waist, Laurent lifted her to the ground. Elizabeth shivered in delight at the feel of his strong hands on her body.

"You handle Cendrillon as if you've been riding horses forever," Laurent said admiringly.

Elizabeth flushed in pleasure. "I've actually been going horseback riding since I was a little girl. It's sort of in my blood."

Laurent lifted an eyebrow. "In your blood?" he questioned.

Elizabeth blushed slightly. "Well, my distant relatives

were, um, acrobats in the circus," she admitted.

Laurent laughed. "That I would have never guessed!" He studied her face carefully. "I might have thought you came from a family of actresses, or dancers, or movie stars—"

"Laurent, stop it!" Elizabeth cut him off. "Flattery will get you nowhere."

Laurent looked at her intensely. "Elizabeth, I am not flattering you."

Elizabeth swallowed hard, feeling her chest tighten suddenly. Laurent already had a dangerously strong hold on her emotions. She stepped away quickly, walking closer to the pond.

Laurent joined her at the edge of the water. For a moment they were silent as they gazed together at the peaceful water.

"This is incredible!" Elizabeth breathed finally. The sky was a deep blue, and the woods were full of night sounds. Crickets were chirping, and leaves were rustling. Elizabeth felt as if she were in a glorious, romantic dream.

Laurent reached for her hand. "This is where I first saw you," he whispered.

Elizabeth frowned. "But I've never seen this pond before," she said. "I'm sure I didn't wander off this far from the château when I got lost."

Laurent chuckled softly. "That's because you weren't here."

"Huh?" Elizabeth asked, turning to him with a puzzled expression.

"I saw you in a dream," he explained softly, giving her hand a squeeze.

Elizabeth's heart skipped a beat. Was it possible? Had Laurent dreamed of her as well?

Laurent let go of her hand and sat down on the bank of the pond. "I fell asleep right on that spot last Sunday," he said, pointing to a clover patch on the bank.

"And what did you dream?" Elizabeth asked softly. She sat down next to him, curling her legs underneath her.

Laurent looked pensive for a moment. "I dreamed I was at some sort of royal ball. From across the room I saw a beautiful girl with golden hair and ocean blue eyes."

Laurent looked at Elizabeth intently, his eyes searching her face. Elizabeth's heart fluttered under the intensity of his gaze, and she looked down quickly.

"I went to her, and I put my arms around her to dance," Laurent continued. Then he sighed. "But then she disappeared."

Elizabeth turned to look at him, smiling slightly.

Laurent gently touched her face. "I never thought I would be lucky enough to meet the beautiful girl who appeared to me that day. But now the dream has come true."

Elizabeth felt a rush of happiness sweep over her body. *Is this really happening?* she asked herself, awed.

For a moment Elizabeth was tempted to tell him about her dream, but then she stopped herself. *For now,* she decided, *I'll keep that secret to myself.* After all, she and Laurent had all summer to discover each other.

Laurent took her chin and lifted her face to his. Then he kissed her softly—a long, sweet, tender kiss. He tangled a hand in her silky hair, and his other hand reached out for hers. At the feel of his strong hand over hers, Elizabeth felt her whole body melt.

Maybe fairy tales can come true, she thought. And then she returned his kiss with a passion so strong, it surprised even her.

"Let me go!" Jessica muttered through clenched teeth, trying to bite at her captor's hand. Her heart pounded like a jackhammer as she tried to pull herself free.

A beam of moonlight peeked through the lace curtains, suddenly illuminating the room. Jessica blinked, trying to make out her surroundings. Then her blood froze in her veins. Her three bureau drawers were open and had been rifled through. *A robbery?* she thought. *Does the thief have a knife? Or a gun?* A bolt of fear shot through her.

Summoning all her energy, she yanked an arm free and elbowed her captor.

A male voice groaned, and two strong arms enfolded her. Jessica struggled wildly, but to no avail.

Her captor's arms felt like solid lead around her. She couldn't move at all. Jessica whimpered in fear.

But then the grip loosened and a voice whispered in her ear, "Jessica, please be still."

A jolt of recognition shot through her at the sound of the sexy voice. Jessica nodded, holding her breath.

The guy turned her around, took his hand away from her mouth, and flicked on the light. It was Jacques, and he looked cuter than ever. His hair was in disarray, and his jaw was covered in a thick stubble. His eyes were wide with worry.

"Jacques!" Jessica uttered breathlessly.

"Jessica," Jacques said softly. "I've found you at last."

Jessica's whole body trembled in relief. She felt suddenly weak and grabbed onto the bureau for support. Then she stared at him in shock, her mind racing. *How did he get in? What is he doing here? Why did he scare me like that?* "Jacques . . . I . . . why—" she began.

But Jacques cut her off. He crossed the room swiftly and grabbed her in his arms. "Jessica," he whispered. Then he pressed his lips against hers. For a moment she resisted, but then she felt herself melting at the sensation of his delicious kiss.

Jacques wrapped his arms tight around her, and his mouth devoured hers hungrily, as if he couldn't get enough. Jessica closed her eyes and returned his embrace with the same ardor.

Finally Jacques pulled back, out of breath. Then he stared at her intensely, his liquid brown eyes on fire. He ran a finger along her cheekbone, a tender look on his face. "I've missed you so," he whispered.

Jessica looked up at him, amazed. She still couldn't quite believe he was here. "But . . . but what are you doing in here?" she stuttered.

Jacques paced across the wooden floor. "I couldn't wait to see you again," he explained. "Ever since I met you, I haven't stopped thinking about you. You're in all my thoughts, in my dreams—"

Jessica's heart fluttered at his words.

"I took the first train I could," he continued. "And as soon as I arrived at the château, I had to find you." He leaned against the bureau. "I didn't want the de Sainte-Maries to know I was here because they'd never let us be alone together." Jacques gave her an intense look and spread his hands out in a wide gesture. "I . . . I desperately wanted to steal a few minutes alone with you."

Jessica sat down on the edge of the bed, trying to make sense of what he was telling her. "But how did you get in?" She gestured toward the stairs. "In case you haven't noticed, there's a major dinner party going on."

Jacques smiled, the familiar rakish look in his eyes. "I have my ways," he said mysteriously.

"The underground passageways?" Jessica guessed.

Jacques nodded. "There's an old, unused dumbwaiter that connects all the floors. I got into the castle through one of the underground routes and then took the dumbwaiter," he explained.

Jessica silently digested the information. But then she frowned. "But why were you going through my bureau?" she asked.

Jacques averted his eyes. "I'm sorry for invading your privacy like that," he said, looking abashed. "But I didn't know if I was in the right room." He paused. "I was looking for something that would indicate this one is yours." He flashed her a sexy smile. "And then you came in."

Jessica nodded. His story made sense, but still, something was bothering her. For a moment she thought about Anna's claim that there was no duke of Norveaux. *Poor Jessica,* she heard Anna's laughing voice saying. *You've run into a dashing French rogue with a silver tongue.*

Jessica squinted, looking at Jacques carefully. His head was lowered, and he looked slightly embarrassed. He returned her gaze, searching her face quickly with wide, sincere eyes.

Anna can't be right, Jessica decided. Obviously Jacques wasn't a rogue like she'd thought. He had come all this way to see her, just as he had promised he would. And that was all that mattered.

"Jessica?" Jacques asked, a question in his voice. "Is something wrong?"

Jessica shook her head, giving him a tiny smile. "No, nothing's wrong," she whispered. "Nothing at all."

Then she slipped back into his arms and stared into his warm eyes. With the moonlight shining on his strong jaw, Jacques bent his face to hers. As their lips met, the whole world seemed to disappear.

This is all that matters, Jessica thought again, and then she lost herself in the searing heat of his kiss.

Don't miss the next two Sweet Valley High Magna Editions, **Elizabeth's Secret Diary, Volume III,** *and* **Jessica's Secret Diary, Volume III.** *Read all about Elizabeth's tortured romance and Jessica's chance at stardom, featuring classic moments from Sweet Valley High books 71–94. If you miss these Magnas, you'll never find out the captivating, unbelievable truth of what really happened during the most turbulent time in the twins' lives!*

Then continue your journey with Jessica and Elizabeth to Château d'Amour Inconnu, the French castle by the sea, for a summer of royalty and romance. The twins may be falling in love, but both their new boyfriends have secrets that may land Elizabeth and Jessica in more trouble than they ever imagined! Don't dare miss Sweet Valley High 133, **To Catch a Thief,** *the second book in an enchanting three-part miniseries— coming soon. It's a fairy tale come true!*

Bantam Books in the Sweet Valley High series
Ask your bookseller for the books you have missed